FAIRY TALES

By HANS ANDERSEN

Illustrated by KAY NIELSEN

H C ANDERSEN

FAIRYTALES

KAY NIELSEN PINXIT

A STUDIO BOOK · THE METROPOLITAN MUSEUM OF ART
AND THE VIKING PRESS · NEW YORK

The illustrations are reproduced from a copy
of the 1924 edition in the collection of
The Metropolitan Museum of Art, a gift of
Mr. and Mrs. Bryan Holme.

Copyright © 1981 by Viking Penguin Inc.
All rights reserved
First published in 1981 by The Viking Press (A Studio Book)
625 Madison Avenue, New York, N.Y. 10022
Published simultaneously in Canada by
Penguin Books Canada Limited

LIBRARY OF CONGRESS CATALOGING IN PUBLICATION DATA
Andersen, H. C. (Hans Christian), 1805–1875.
Fairy tales.
(A Studio book)
Contents: The tinder box—The real princess—
The elder tree mother—[etc.]
1. Fairy tales, Danish.   2. Children's stories,
Danish—Translations into English.   3. Children's
stories, English—Translation from Danish. [1. Fairy
tales] I. Nielsen, Kay Rasmus, 1886–1957. II. Title.
PZ8.A54 1981   [Fic]   81-43012
ISBN 0-670-30557-X   AACR2

Printed in the United States of America
Color plates printed in Japan by Dai Nippon Printing Co., Ltd., Tokyo

Contents

Illustrations

THE · TINDER · BOX

HERE came a soldier marching along the high road—*one, two! one, two!* He had his knapsack on his back and a sabre by his side, for he had been in the wars, and now he wanted to go home. And on the way he met with an old witch : she was very hideous, and her under lip hung down upon her breast. She said, " Good evening, soldier. What a fine sword you have, and what a big knapsack ! You're a proper soldier ! Now you shall have as much money as you like to have."

" I thank you, you old witch ! " said the soldier.

" Do you see that great tree ? " quoth the witch ; and she pointed to a tree which stood beside them. " It's quite hollow inside. You must climb to the top, and then you'll see a hole, through which you can let yourself down and get deep into the tree. I'll tie a rope round your body, so that I can pull you up again when you call me."

" What am I to do down in the tree ? " asked the soldier. " Get money," replied the witch. " Listen to me. When you come down to the earth under the tree, you will find yourself in a great hall : it is quite light, for many hundred lamps are burning there. Then you will see three doors ; these you can open, for the keys are in the locks. If you go into the first chamber, you'll see a great chest in the middle of the floor ; on this chest sits a dog, and he's got a pair of eyes as big as two tea cups. But you need not care for that. I'll give you my blue-checked apron, and you can spread it out upon the floor ; then go up quickly and take the dog, and set him on my apron ; then open the chest, and take as many farthings as you like. They are of copper : if you prefer silver, you must go into the second chamber. But there sits a dog with a pair of eyes as big as mill wheels. But do not you care for that. Set him upon my apron, and take some of the money. And if you want gold, you can have that, too—in fact, as much as you can carry—if you go into the third chamber. But the dog that sits on the money-chest there has two eyes as big as the round tower of Copenhagen. He is a fierce dog, you may be sure, but you needn't be afraid, for all that. Only set him on my apron, and he won't hurt you ; and take out of the chest as much gold as you like."

"That's not so bad," said the soldier. "But what am I to give you, you old witch ? for you will not do it for nothing, I fancy."

"No," replied the witch, "not a single farthing will I have. You shall only bring me an old-tinder box which my grandmother forgot when she was down there last."

"Then tie the rope round my body," cried the soldier.

"Here it is," said the witch, "and here's my blue-checked apron."

Then the soldier climbed up into the tree, let himself slip down into the hole, and stood, as the witch had said, in the great hall where the many hundred lamps were burning.

Now he opened the first door. Ugh ! there sat the dog with eyes as big as tea cups, staring at him. "You're a nice fellow !" exclaimed the soldier ; and he set him on the witch's apron, and took as many copper farthings as his pockets would hold, and then locked the chest, set the dog on it again, and went into the second chamber. Aha ! there sat the dog with eyes as big as mill wheels.

" You should not stare so hard at me," said the soldier ; " you might strain your eyes." And he set the dog upon the witch's apron. When he saw the silver money in the chest, he threw away all the copper money he had, and filled his pockets and his knapsack with silver only. Then he went into the third chamber. Oh, but that was horrid ! The dog there really had eyes as big as the round tower, and they turned round and round in his head like wheels.

" Good evening " said the soldier ; and he touched his cap, for he had never seen such a dog as that before. When he had looked at him a little more closely, he thought, " That will do," and lifted him down to the floor, and opened the chest. Mercy ! what a quantity of gold was there ! He could buy with it the whole of Copenhagen, and the sugar-pigs of the cake-woman, and all the tin soldiers, whips, and rocking-horses in the whole world. Yes, that was a quantity of money ! Now the soldier threw away all the silver coin with which he had filled his pockets and his knapsack, and took gold instead : yes, all his pockets, his knapsack, his boots, and his cap were filled, so that he could scarcely walk. Now, indeed, he had plenty of money. He put the dog on the chest, shut the door, and then called up through the tree, " Now pull me up, you old witch."

" Have you the tinder box ? " asked the witch.

" Plague on it ! " exclaimed the soldier, " I had clean forgotten that." And he went and brought it.

The witch drew him up, and he stood on the high road again, with pockets, boots, knapsack, and cap full of gold.

" What are you going to do with the tinder box ? " asked the soldier.

" That's nothing to you," retorted the witch. " You've had your money—just give me the tinder box."

" Nonsense ! " said the soldier. " Tell me directly what you're going to do with it, or I'll draw my sword and cut off your head."

" No ! " cried the witch.

So the soldier cut off her head. There she lay ! But he tied up all his money in her apron, took it on his back like a bundle, put the tinder box in his pocket, and went straight off towards the town.

That was a splendid town ! He put up at the very best inn, asked for the finest rooms, and ordered his favourite dishes, for now he was rich, having got so much money. The servant who had to clean his boots certainly thought them a remarkably old pair for such a rich gentleman ; but he had not bought any new ones yet. The next day he procured proper boots and handsome clothes. Now our soldier had become a fine gentleman ; and the people told him of all the splendid things which were in their city, and about the king, and what a pretty princess the king's daughter was.

" Where can one get to see her ? " asked the soldier.

" She is not to be seen at all," said they all together ; she lives in a great copper castle, with a great many walls and towers round about it ; no one but the king may go in and out there, for it has been prophesied that she shall marry a common soldier, and the king can't bear that.

" I should like to see her," thought the soldier ; but he could not get leave to do so. Now he lived merrily, went to the theatre, drove in the king's garden, and gave much money to the poor ; and this was very kind of him, for he knew from old times how hard it is when one has not a shilling. Now he was rich, had fine clothes, and gained many friends, who all said he was a rare one, a true cavalier ; and that pleased the soldier well. But as he spent money every day and never earned any, he had at last only two shillings left ; and he was obliged to turn out of the fine rooms in which he had dwelt, and had to live in a little garret under the roof, and clean his boots for himself, and mend them with a darning-needle. None of his friends came to see him, for there were too many stairs to climb.

It was quite dark one evening, and he could not even buy himself a candle, when it occured to him that there was a candle-end in the tinder box which he had taken out of the hollow tree into which the witch had helped him. He brought out the tinder box and the candle-end ; but as soon as he struck fire and the sparks rose up from the flint, the door flew open, and the dog who had eyes as big as a couple of tea cups, and whom he had seen in the tree, stood before him, and said,

" What are my lord's commands ? "

" What is this ? " said the soldier. " That's a famous tinder box, if I can get everything with it that I want ! Bring me some money," said he to the dog ; and *whisk !* the dog was gone, and *whisk !* he was back again, with a great bag full of shillings in his mouth.

Now the soldier knew what a capital tinder box this was. If he struck it once, the dog came who sat upon the chest of copper money ; if he struck it twice, the dog came who had the silver ; and if he struck it three times, then appeared the dog who had the gold. Now the soldier moved back into the fine rooms, and appeared again in handsome clothes ; and all his friends knew him again, and cared very much for him indeed.

Once he thought to himself, " It is a very strange thing that one cannot get to see the princess. They all say she is very beautiful ; but what is the use of that, if she has always to sit in the great copper castle with the many towers ? Can I not get to see her at all ? Where is my tinder box ? " And so he struck a light, and *whisk !* came the dog with eyes as big as tea cups.

" It is midnight, certainly," said the soldier, " but I should very much like to see the princess, only for one little moment."

13

THE TINDER BOX

The dog was outside the door directly, and, before the soldier thought it, came back with the princess. She sat upon the dog's back and slept; and every one could see she was a real princess, for she was so lovely. The soldier could not refrain from kissing her, for he was a thorough soldier. Then the dog ran back again with the princess. But when morning came, and the king and queen were drinking tea, the princess said she had had a strange dream the night before, about a dog and a soldier—that she had ridden upon the dog, and the soldier had kissed her.

"That would be a fine history!" said the Queen.

So one of the old court ladies had to watch the next night by the princess's bed, to see if this was really a dream, or what it might be.

The soldier had a great longing to see the lovely princess again; so the dog came in the night, took her away, and ran as fast as he could. But the old lady put on water-boots, and ran just as fast after him. When she saw that they both entered a great house, she thought, "Now I know where it is;" and with a bit of chalk she drew a great cross on the door. Then she went home and lay down, and the dog came up with the princess; but when he saw that there was a cross drawn on the door where the soldier lived, he took a piece of chalk, too, and drew crosses on all the doors in the town. And that was cleverly done, for now the lady could not find the right door, because all the doors had crosses upon them.

In the morning early came the King and the Queen, the old court lady and all the officers, to see where it was the princess had been. "Here it is!" said the King, when he saw the first door with a cross upon it. "No, my dear husband, it is there!" said the Queen, who descried another door which also showed a cross. "But *there* is one, and *there* is one!" said all, for wherever they looked there were crosses on the doors. So they saw that it would avail them nothing if they searched on.

But the Queen was an exceedingly clever woman, who could do more than ride in a coach. She took her great gold scissors, cut a piece of silk into pieces, and made a neat little bag ; this bag she filled with fine wheat flour, and tied it on the princess's back ; and when that was done, she cut a little hole in the bag, so that the flour would be scattered along all the way which the princess should take.

In the night the dog came again, took the princess on his back, and ran with her to the soldier, who loved her very much, and would gladly have been a prince, so that he might have married her. The dog did not notice at all how the flour ran out in a stream from the castle to the windows of the soldier's house, where he ran up the wall with the princess. In the morning the King and the Queen saw well enough where their daughter had been, and they took the soldier and put him in prison.

There he sat. Oh, but it was dark and disagreeable there ! And they said to him, "To-morrow you shall be hanged." That was not amusing to hear, and he had left his tinder box at the inn. In the morning he could see, through the iron grating of the little window, how the people were hurrying out of the town to see him hanged. He heard the drums beat and saw the soldiers marching. All the people were running out, and among them was a shoemaker's boy with leather apron and slippers, and he galloped so fast that one of his slippers flew off, and came right against the wall where the soldier sat looking through the iron grating.

"Halloo, you shoemaker's boy ! you needn't be in such a hurry," cried the soldier to him · " it will not begin till I come. But if you will run to where I lived, and bring me my tinder box, you shall have four shillings ; but you must put your best leg foremost."

THE TINDER BOX

The shoemaker's boy wanted to get the four shillings, so he went and brought the tinder box, and—well, we shall hear now what happened.

Outside the town a great gallows had been built, and round it stood the soldiers and many hundred thousand people. The King and Queen sat on a splendid throne, opposite to the judges and the whole council. The soldier already stood upon the ladder; but as they were about to put the rope round his neck, he said that before a poor criminal suffered his punishment an innocent request was always granted to him. He wanted very much to smoke a pipe of tobacco, and it would be the last pipe he should smoke in the world. The king would not say " No " to this; so the soldier took his tinder box, and struck fire. One—two—three !—and there suddenly stood all the dogs—the one with eyes as big as tea cups, the one with eyes as large as mill-wheels, and the one whose eyes were as big as the round tower.

" Help me now, so that I may not be hanged," said the soldier.

And the dogs fell upon the judge and all the council, seized one by the leg and another by the nose, and tossed them all many feet into the air, so that they fell down and were all broken to pieces.

" I won't ! " cried the King; but the biggest dog took him and the Queen, and threw them after the others. Then the soldiers were afraid, and the people cried, " Little soldier, you shall be our king, and marry the beautiful princess ! "

So they put the soldier into the king's coach, and all the three dogs danced in front and cried " Hurrah ! " and the boys whistled through their fingers, and the soldiers presented arms. The princess came out of the copper castle, and became queen, and she liked that well enough. The wedding lasted a week, and the three dogs sat at the table too, and opened their eyes wider than ever at all they saw.

In the night the dog came again, took the princess on his back and ran with her to the soldier. - - - - - - - *p.* 15

NCE there was a Prince who wished to marry a Princess; but then she must be a real Princess. He travelled all over the world in hopes of finding such a lady; but there was always something wrong. Princesses he found in plenty; but whether they were real Princesses it was impossible for him to decide, for now one thing, now another, seemed to him not quite right about the ladies. At last he returned to his palace quite cast down, because he wished so much to have a real Princess for his wife.

One evening a fearful tempest arose; it thundered and lightened, and the rain poured down from the sky in torrents; besides, it was as dark as pitch. All at once there was heard a violent knocking at the door, and the old King, the Prince's father, went out himself to open it.

It was a Princess who was standing outside the door. What with the rain and the wind, she was in a sad condition: the water trickled down from her hair, and her clothes clung to her body. She said she was a real Princess.

"Ah, we shall soon see that!" thought the old Queen-mother; however, she said not a word of what she was going to do, but went quietly into the bedroom, took all the bedclothes off the bed, and put three little peas on the bedstead. She then laid twenty mattresses one upon another over the three peas, and put twenty feather-beds over the mattresses.

"Oh very badly indeed!" she replied. "I have scarcely closed my eyes the whole night through. I do not know what was in my bed." *p.* 20

19

THE REAL PRINCESS

Upon this bed the Princess was to pass the night.

The next morning she was asked how she had slept. "Oh, very badly indeed!" she replied. "I have scarcely closed my eyes the whole night through. I do not know what was in my bed, but I had something hard under me, and am all over black and blue. It has hurt me so much!"

Now it was plain that the lady must be a real Princess, since she had been able to feel the three little peas through the twenty mattresses and twenty feather-beds. None but a real Princess could have had such a delicate sense of feeling.

The Prince accordingly made her his wife, being now convinced that he had found a real Princess. The three peas were, however, put into the cabinet of curiosities, where they are still to be seen, provided they are not lost.

Was not this a lady of real delicacy?

THE · ELDER · TREE · MOTHER

HERE was once a little boy who had caught cold ; he had gone out and got wet feet ; no one could imagine how it had happened, for it was quite dry weather.   Now his mother undressed him, put him to bed, and had the tea-urn brought in to make him a good cup of elder tea, for that warms well.   At the same time there also came in at the door the friendly old man who lived all alone at the top of the house, and was very solitary.   He had neither wife nor children, but he was very fond of all children, and knew so many stories that it was quite delightful.

" Now you are to drink your tea," said the mother, " and then perhaps you will hear a story."

" Ah ! if one only could tell a new one ! " said the old man, with a friendly nod.   " But where did the little man get his feet wet ? " he asked.

" Yes," replied the mother, " no one can imagine how that came about."

" Shall I have a story ? " asked the boy.

" Yes, if you can tell me at all accurately—for I must know that first—how deep the gutter is in the little street through which you go to school."

" Just half-way up to my knee," answered the boy, " that is, if I put my feet in the deep hole."

THE ELDER TREE MOTHER

" You see, that's how we get our feet wet," said the old gentleman. " Now I ought certainly to tell you a story ; but I don't know any more."

" You can make up one directly," answered the little boy. " Mother says that everything you look at can be turned into a story, and that you can make a tale of everything you touch."

" Yes, but those stories and tales are worth nothing ! No, the real ones come of themselves. They knock at my forehead, and say, Here I am ! "

" Will there soon be a knock ? " asked the little boy, and the mother laughed, and put elder tea in the pot, and poured hot water upon it.

" A story ! a story ! "

" Yes, if a story would come of itself ; but that kind of thing is very grand ; it only comes when it's in the humour.—Wait ! " he cried all at once ; " here we have it. Look you ; there's one in the tea-pot now."

And the little boy looked across at the tea-pot. The lid raised itself more and more, and the elder flowers came forth from it, white and fresh ; they shot forth long fresh branches even out of the spout, they spread abroad in all directions, and became larger and larger ; there was the most glorious elder bush—in fact, quite a great tree. It penetrated even to the bed, and thrust the curtains aside ; how fragrant it was, and how it bloomed ! And in the midst of the tree sat an old, pleasant-looking woman in a strange dress. It was quite green, like the leaves of the elder tree, and bordered with great white elder blossoms ; one could not at once discern whether this border was of stuff or of living green and real flowers.

" What is the woman's name ? " the little boy asked.

" The Romans and Greeks," replied the old man, " used to call her a Dryad ; but we don't understand that : out in the

26

sailors' quarter we have a better name for her ; there she's called Elder Tree Mother, and it is to her you must pay attention ; only listen, and look at that glorious elder tree."

"Just such a great blooming tree stands out in the sailors' quarter ; it grew there in the corner of a poor little yard, and under this tree two old people sat one afternoon in the brightest sunshine. It was an old, old sailor, and his old, old wife ; they had great-grandchildren, and were soon to celebrate their golden wedding ; but they could not quite make out the date, and the Elder Tree Mother sat in the tree and looked pleased, just as she does here. 'I know very well when the golden wedding is to be,' said she ; but they did not hear it—they were talking of old times."

"'Yes, do you remember,'" said the old seaman, 'when we were quite little, and ran about and played together ! It was in the very same yard where we are sitting now, and we planted little twigs in the yard, and made a garden.'"

"Yes," replied the old woman, "I remember it very well : we watered the twigs, and one of them was an elder twig ; that struck root, shot out other green twigs, and has become the great tree, under which we old people sit."

"Surely," said he ; "and yonder in the corner stood a butt of water ; there I swam my boat ; I had cut it out myself. How it could sail ! But I certainly soon had to sail in a different fashion myself."

"But first we went to school and learned something," said she, "and then we were confirmed ; we both cried, but in the afternoon we went hand in hand to the round tower, and looked out into the wide world, over Copenhagen and across the water ; then we went out to Fredericksberg, where the King and Queen were sailing in their splendid boats upon the canals."

"But I was obliged to sail in another fashion, and that for

many years, far away on long voyages."

"Yes, I often cried about you," she said. "I thought you were dead and gone, and lying down in the deep waters, rocked by the waves. Many a night I got up to look if the weathercock was turning. Yes, it turned indeed ; but you did not come. I remember so clearly how the rain streamed down one day. The man with the cart who fetched away the dust came to the place where I was in service. I went down to him with the dust-bin, and remained standing in the doorway. What wretched weather it was ! And just as I stood there the postman came up and gave me a letter. It was from you ! How that letter had travelled about ! I tore it open and read ; I laughed and wept at once, I was so glad. There it stood written that you were in the warm countries where the coffee-beans grow. What a delightful land that must be ! You told me so much, and I read it all while the rain was streaming down, and I stood by the dust-bin. Then somebody came and clasped me round the waist."

"And you gave him a terrible box on the ear—one that sounded ? "

"I did not know that it was you. You had arrived just as quickly as your letter. And you were so handsome ; but that you are still. You had a long yellow silk handkerchief in your pocket, and a shiny hat on your head. You were so handsome ! And, gracious ! what weather it was, and how the street looked ! "

"Then we were married," said he ; "do you remember ? And then when our first little boy came, and then Marie, and Neils, and Peter and Hans Christian ? "

"Yes, and how all of these have grown up to be respectable people, and every one likes them."

"And their children have had little ones in their turn," said the old sailor. "Yes, those are children's children ! They're of the right sort. It was, if I don't mistake, at this very season of the year that we were married ? "

" Yes ; this is the day of your golden wedding," said the Elder Tree Mother, putting out her head just between the two old people ; and they thought it was a neighbour nodding to them, and they looked at each other, and took hold of one another's hands.

Soon afterwards came their children and grandchildren ; these knew very well that it was the golden wedding-day ; they had already brought their congratulations in the morning, but the old people had forgotten it, while they remembered everything right well that had happened years and years ago.

And the elder tree smelt so strong, and the sun that was just setting shone just in the faces of the old people, so that their cheeks looked quite red ; and the youngest of their grandchildren danced about them, and cried out quite gleefully that there was to be a feast this evening, for they were to have hot potatoes ; and the Elder Mother nodded in the tree, and called out " hurrah ! " with all the rest.

" But that was not a story," said the little boy who had heard it told.

" Yes, if you could understand it," replied the old man ; " but let us ask the Elder Mother about it."

" That was not a story," said the Elder Mother ; " but now it comes ; but of truth the strangest stories are formed, otherwise my beautiful elder tree could not have sprouted forth out of the tea-pot."

And then she took the little boy out of bed, and laid him upon her bosom, and the blossoming elder branches wound round them, so that they sat as it were in the thickest arbour, and this arbour flew with them through the air. It was indescribably beautiful. Elder Mother all at once became a pretty young girl ; but her dress was still of the green stuff with the white blossoms that

THE ELDER TREE MOTHER

Elder Mother had worn; in her bosom she had a real elder
blossom, and about her yellow curly hair a wreath of elder flowers;
her eyes were so large and blue, they were beautiful to look at.
She and the boy were of the same age, and they kissed each other
and felt similar joys.

Hand in hand they went forth out of the arbour, and now they
stood in the beauteous flower garden of home. The father's staff
was tied up near the fresh grass-plot, and for the little boy there
was life in that staff. As soon as they seated themselves upon it,
the polished head turned into a noble neighing horse's head, with
a flowing mane, and four slender legs shot forth; the creature
was strong and spirited, and they rode at a gallop round the
grass-plot—hurrah!

"Now we're going to ride many miles away," said the boy;
"we'll ride to the nobleman's estate, where we went last year!"

And they rode round and round the grass-plot, and the little
girl, who, as we know, was no one else but Elder Mother, kept
crying out.

"Now we're in the country! Do you see the farmhouse,
with the great baking-oven standing out of the wall like an
enormous egg by the wayside? The elder tree spreads its
branches over it, and the cock walks about, scratching for his
hens; look how he struts! Now we are near the church; it
lies high up on the hill, among the great oak trees, one of which
is half dead. Now we are at the forge, where the fire burns and
the half-clad men beat with their hammers, so that the sparks fly
far around. Away, away to the nobleman's splendid seat!"

And everything that the little maiden mentioned, as she sat on
the stick behind him, flew past them, and the little boy saw it all,
though they were only riding round and round the grass-plot.
Then they played in the side-walk, and scratched up the earth to
make a little garden; and she took elder flowers out of her hair

and planted them, and they grew just like those that the old people had planted when they were little, as has been already told. They went hand in hand just as the old people had done in their childhood ; but not to the round tower, or to the Fredericksberg Garden.   No, the little girl took hold of the boy round the body, and then they flew here and there over the whole of Denmark.

And it was spring, and summer came, and autumn, and winter, and thousands of pictures were mirrored in the boy's eyes and heart, and the little maiden was always singing to him.

He will never forget that ; and throughout their whole journey the elder tree smelt so sweet, so fragrant ; he noticed the roses and the fresh beech trees ; but the elder tree smelt stronger than all, for its flowers hung round the little girl's heart, and he often leaned against them as they flew onward.

" How beautiful it is here in spring ! " said the little girl.

And they stood in the new-leaved beech wood, where the green woodruff lay spread in fragrance at their feet, and the pale pink anemones looked glorious among the vivid green.

" Oh, that it were always spring in the fragrant Danish beech woods ! "

" How beautiful it is here in summer ! " said she.

And they passed by old castles of knightly days, castles whose red walls and pointed gables were mirrored in the canals, where swans swam about, and looked down the old shady avenues.   In the fields the corn waved like a sea, in the ditches yellow and red flowers were growing, and in the hedges wild hops and blooming convolvulus.   In the evening the moon rose round and large, and the haystacks in the meadows smelt sweet.

" How beautiful it is here in autumn ! " said the little girl.

And the sky seemed twice as lofty and twice as blue as before, and the forest was decked in the most gorgeous tints of red, yellow, and green.   The hunting dogs raced about ; whole flocks of wild ducks flew screaming over the ancient grave-mound, on which bramble bushes twined over the old stones. The sea was dark blue, and covered with ships and white sails ; and in the barns sat old women, girls, and children, picking hops into a large tub : the young people sang songs, and the older ones told tales of magicians and goblins. It could not be finer anywhere.

" How beautiful it is here in winter ! " said the little girl.

And all the trees were covered with hoar frost, so that they looked like white trees of coral. The snow crackled beneath one's feet, as if every one had new boots on ; and one shooting star after another fell from the sky. In the room the Christmas tree was lighted up, and there were presents, and there was happiness. In the country people's farmhouses the violin sounded, and there were merry games for apples ; and even the poorest child said, " It is beautiful in winter ! "

Yes, it was beautiful ; and the little girl showed the boy everything ; and still the blossoming tree smelt sweet, and still waved the red flag with the white cross, the flag under which the old seaman had sailed. The boy became a youth, and was to go out into the wide world, far away to the hot countries where the coffee grows. But when they were to part the little girl took an elder blossom from her breast, and gave it to him to keep. It was laid in his hymn-book, and in the foreign land, when he opened the book, it was always at the place where the flower of remembrance lay ; and the more he looked at the flower the fresher it became, so that he seemed, as it were, to breathe the forest air of home ; then he plainly saw the little girl looking out with her clear blue eyes from between the petals of the flower, and then she whispered, " How beautiful it is here in spring, summer, autumn, and winter ! " and hundreds of pictures glided through his thoughts.

Thus many years went by, and now he was an old man, and

sat with his old wife under the blossoming elder tree : they were holding each other by the hand, just as the great-grandmother and great-grandfather had done before ; and, like these, they spoke of old times and of the golden wedding. The little maiden with the blue eyes and with the elder blossoms in her hair sat up in the tree, and nodded to both of them, and said, " To-day is the golden wedding-day ! " and then she took two flowers out of her hair and kissed them, and they gleamed first like silver and then like gold, and when she laid them on the heads of the old people each changed into a golden crown. There they both sat, like a King and a Queen, under the fragrant tree which looked quite like an elder bush, and he told his old wife of the story of the Elder Tree Mother, as it had been told to him when he was quite a little boy, and they both thought that there was so much in the story that resembled their own, and those parts they liked the best.

" Yes, thus it is ! " said the little girl in the tree. " Some call me Elder Tree Mother, others the Dryad, but my real name is Remembrance : it is I who sit in the tree that grows on and on, and I can think back and tell stories. Let me see if you have still your flower."

And the old man opened his hymn-book ; there lay the elder blossom as fresh as if it had only just been placed there ; and Remembrance nodded, and the two old people with the golden crowns on their heads sat in the red evening sunlight, and they closed their eyes, and—and—the story was finished.

The little boy lay in his bed and did not know whether he had been dreaming or had heard a tale told ; the tea-pot stood on the table, but no elder bush was growing out of it, and the old man who had told about it was just going out of the door, and indeed he went.

" How beautiful that was ! " said the little boy. " Mother I have been in the hot countries."

THE ELDER TREE MOTHER

" Yes, I can imagine that ! " replied his mother. " When one drinks two cups of hot elder tea one very often gets into the hot countries ! " And she covered him up well, that he might not take cold. " You have slept well while I disputed with him as to whether it was a story or a fairy tale."

" And where is the Elder Tree Mother ? " asked the little lad.

" She's in the teapot," replied his mother ; " and there she may stay."

And in the midst of the tree sat an old, pleasant-looking woman in a strange dress. -   -   -   -   -   -   -   -   *p.* 26

34

And when I get back and am tired, and rest in the wood, then I hear the Nightingale sing. - - - - - - - *p.* 41

THE · NIGHTINGALE

N China, you must know, the Emperor is a Chinaman, and all whom he has about him are Chinamen too. It happened a good many years ago, but that's just why it's worth while to hear the story, before it is forgotten. The Emperor's palace was the most splendid in the world ; it was made entirely of porcelain, very costly, but so delicate and brittle that one had to take care how one touched it. In the garden were to be seen the most wonderful flowers, and to the costliest of them silver bells were tied, which sounded, so that nobody should pass by without noticing the flowers. Yes, everything in the Emperor's garden was admirably arranged. And it extended so far, that the gardener himself did not know where the end was. If a man went on and on, he came into a glorious forest with high trees and deep lakes. The wood extended straight down to the sea, which was blue and deep ; great ships could sail in beneath the branches of the trees ; and in the trees lived a Nightingale, which sang so splendidly that even the poor fisherman, who had many other things to do, stopped still and listened, when he had gone out at night to take up his nets, and heard the Nightingale.

"How beautiful that is !" he said ; but he was obliged to attend to his business, and thus forgot the bird. But when in the next night the bird sang again, and the fisherman heard it, he

39

exclaimed again, " how beautiful that is ! "

From all the countries of the world travellers came to the city of the Emperor, and admired it, and the palace and the garden, but when they heard the Nightingale, they said, " That is the best of all ! "

And the travellers told of it when they came home ; and the learned men wrote many books about the town, the palace and the garden. But they did not forget the Nightingale ; that was placed highest of all ; and those who were poets wrote most magnificent poems about the Nightingale in the wood by the deep lake.

The books went through all the world, and a few of them once came to the Emperor. He sat in his golden chair, and read, and read : every moment he nodded his head, for it pleased him to peruse the masterly descriptions of the city, the palace, and the garden. " But the Nightingale is the best of all," it stood written there.

" What's that ? " exclaimed the Emperor. "I don't know the Nightingale at all ! Is there such a bird in my empire, and even in my garden ? I've never heard of that. To think that I should have to learn such a thing for the first time from books ! "

And hereupon he called his cavalier. This cavalier was so grand that if any one lower in rank than himself dared to speak to him, or to ask him any question, he answered nothing but " P ! "—and that meant nothing.

" There is said to be a wonderful bird here called a Nightingale ! " said the Emperor. " They say it is the best thing in all my great empire. Why have I never heard anything about it ! "

" I have never heard him named," replied the cavalier. " He has never been introduced at court."

" I command that he shall appear this evening, and sing before me," said the Emperor. " All the world knows what I possess, and I do not know it myself ! "

" I have never heard him mentioned," said the cavalier. " I will seek for him. I will find him."

But where was he to be found ? The cavalier ran up and down all the staircases, through halls and passages, but no one among all those whom he met had heard talk of the nightingale. And the cavalier ran back to the Emperor, and said that it must be a fable invented by the writers of books.

" Your Imperial Majesty cannot believe how much is written that is fiction, besides something that they call the black art."

" But the book in which I read this," said the Emperor, " was sent to me by the high and mighty Emperor of Japan, and therefore it cannot be a falsehood. I *will* hear the Nightingale ! It must be here this evening ! It has my imperial favour ; and if it does not come, all the court shall be trampled upon after the court has supped ! "

" Tsing-pe ! " said the cavalier ; and again he ran up and down all the staircases, and through all the halls and corridors ; and half the court ran with him, for the courtiers did not like being trampled upon.

Then there was a great inquiry after the wonderful Nightingale, which all the world knew excepting the people at court.

At last they met with a poor little girl in the kitchen, who said,

" The Nightingale ? I know it well ; yes, it can sing gloriously. Every evening I get leave to carry my poor sick mother the scraps from the table. She lives down by the strand, and when I get back and am tired, and rest in the wood, then I hear the Nightingale sing. And then the water comes into my eyes, and it is just as if my mother kissed me ! "

" Little girl," said the cavalier, " I will get you a place in the kitchen, with permission to see the Emperor dine, if you will lead us to the Nightingale, for it is announced for this evening."

41

THE NIGHTINGALE

So they all went out into the wood where the Nightingale was accustomed to sing ; half the court went forth. When they were in the midst of their journey a cow began to low.

" Oh ! " cried the court page, " now we have it ! That shows a wonderful power in so small a creature ! I have certainly heard it before."

" No, those are cows lowing ! " said the little kitchen-girl. " We are a long way from the place yet."

Now the frogs began to croak in the marsh.

" Glorious ! " said the Chinese court preacher. " Now I hear it—it sounds just like little church bells."

" No, those are frogs ! " said the little kitchen-maid. " But now I think we shall soon hear it."

And then the Nightingale began to sing.

" That is it ! " exclaimed the little girl. " Listen, listen ! and yonder it sits."

And she pointed to a little grey bird up in the boughs.

" Is it possible ? " cried the cavalier. " I should never have thought it looked like that ! How plain it looks ! It must certainly have lost its colour at seeing such grand people around."

" Little Nightingale ! " called the little kitchen-maid, quite loudly, " our gracious Emperor wishes you to sing before him."

" With the greatest pleasure ! " replied the Nightingale, and began to sing most delightfully.

" It sounds just like glass bells ! " said the cavalier. " And look at its little throat, how it's working ! It's wonderful that we should never have heard it before. That bird will be a great success at court."

" Shall I sing once more before the Emperor ? " asked the Nightingale, for it thought the Emperor was present.

" My excellent little Nightingale," said the cavalier, " I have great pleasure in inviting you to a court festival this evening, when you shall charm his Imperial Majesty with your beautiful singing."

"My song sounds best in the green wood!" replied the Nightingale; still it came willingly when it heard what the Emperor wished.

The palace was festively adorned. The walls and the flooring, which were of porcelain, gleamed in the rays of thousands of golden lamps. The most glorious flowers, which could ring clearly, had been placed in the passages. There was a running to and fro, and a thorough draught, and all the bells rang so loudly that one could not hear oneself speak.

In the midst of the great hall, where the Emperor sat, a golden perch had been placed, on which the Nightingale was to sit. The whole court was there, and the little kitchen-maid had got leave to stand behind the door, as she had now received the title of a real court cook. All were in full dress, and all looked at the little grey bird, to which the Emperor nodded.

And the Nightingale sang so gloriously that the tears came into the Emperor's eyes, and the tears ran down over his cheeks; and then the Nightingale sang still more sweetly, so that its song went straight to the heart. The Emperor was so much pleased that he said the Nightingale should have his golden slipper to wear round its neck. But the Nightingale declined this with thanks, saying it had already received a sufficient reward.

"I have seen tears in the Emperor's eyes—that is the real treasure to me. An Emperor's tears have a peculiar power. I am rewarded enough!" And then it sang again with a sweet glorious voice.

"That's the most amiable coquetry I ever saw!" said the ladies who stood round about, and then they took water in their mouths to gurgle when anyone spoke to them. They thought they should be nightingales too. And the lackeys and chambermaids reported that they were satisfied too ; and that was saying a good deal, for they are the most difficult to please. In short, the Nightingale achieved a real success.

It was now to remain at court, to have its own cage, with liberty to go out twice every day and once at night. Twelve servants were appointed when the Nightingale went out, each of whom had a silken string fastened to the bird's leg, and which they held very tight. There was really no pleasure in an excursion of that kind.

The whole city spoke of the wonderful bird, and when two people met, one said nothing but " Nightin," and the other " gale " ; and then they sighed, and understood one another. Eleven pedlars' children were named after the bird, but not one of them could sing a note.

One day the Emperor received a large parcel, on which was written " The Nightingale."

" There we have a new book about this celebrated bird," said the Emperor.

But it was not a book, but a little work of art, contained in a box, an artificial nightingale, which was to sing like the natural one, and was brilliantly ornamented with diamonds, rubies, and sapphires. So soon as the artificial bird was wound up, he could sing one of the pieces that the real one sang, and then his tail moved up and down, and shone with silver and gold. Round his neck hung a little ribbon, and on that was written, " The Emperor of Japan's nightingale is poor compared to that of the Emperor of China."

" That is capital ! " said they all, and he who had brought the artificial bird immediately received the title, Imperial Head-Nightingale-Bringer.

" Now they must sing together ; what a duet that will be ! "

And so they had to sing together ; but it did not sound very well, for the real Nightingale sang in its own way, and the artificial bird sang waltzes.

" That's not his fault," said the playmaster ; " he's quite perfect, and very much in my style."

Now the artificial bird was to sing alone. He had just as much success as the real one, and then it was much handsomer to look at—it shone like bracelets and breastpins.

Three and thirty times over did it sing the same piece, and yet was not tired. The people would gladly have heard it again, but the Emperor said that the living Nightingale ought to sing something now. But where was it ? No one had noticed that it had flown away out of the open window, back to the green wood.

" But what in all the world is this ? " said the Emperor. And all the courtiers abused the Nightingale, and declared that it was a very ungrateful creature.

" We have the best bird, after all," said they.

And so the artificial bird had to sing again, and that was the thirty-fourth time that they listened to the same piece. For all that they did not know it quite by heart, for it was so very difficult. And the playmaster praised the bird particularly ; yes, he declared that it was better than a nightingale, not only with regard to its plumage and the many beautiful diamonds, but inside as well.

" For you see, ladies and gentlemen, and above all, your Imperial Majesty, with a real nightingale one can never calculate what is coming, but in this artificial bird everything is settled. One can explain it ; one can open it and make people understand where the waltzes come from, how they go, and how one follows up another."

" Those are quite our own ideas," they all said.

And the speaker received permission to show the bird to the

people on the next Sunday. The people were to hear it sing too, the Emperor commanded ; and they did hear it, and were as much pleased as if they had all got tipsy upon tea, for that's quite the Chinese fashion ; and they all said, " Oh ! " and held up their forefingers and nodded. But the poor fisherman who had heard the real Nightingale, said

" It sounds pretty enough, and the melodies resemble each other, but there's something wanting, though I know not what ! "

The real Nightingale was banished from the country and empire. The artificial bird had its place on a silken cushion close to the Emperor's bed ; all the presents it had received, gold and precious stones, were ranged about it ; in title it had advanced to be the High Imperial Night-Singer, and in rank to number one on the left hand ; for the Emperor considered that side the most important on which the heart is placed, and even in an Emperor the heart is on the left side ; and the playmaster wrote a work of five-and-twenty volumes about the artificial bird ; it was very learned and very long, full of the most difficult Chinese words ; but yet all the people declared that they had read it and understood it, for fear of being considered stupid, and having their bodies trampled on.

So a whole year went by. The Emperor, the court, and all the other Chinese knew every little twitter in the artificial bird's song by heart. But just for that reason it pleased them best— they could sing with it themselves, and they did so. The street boys sang, " Tsi-tsi-tsi-glug-glug ! " and the Emperor himself sang it too. Yes, that was certainly famous.

But one evening, when the artificial bird was singing its best, and the Emperor lay in bed listening to it, something inside the bird said, " Whizz ! " Something cracked. " Whir-r-r ! " All the wheels ran round, and then the music stopped.

The Emperor immediately sprang out of bed, and caused his

body physician to be called ; but what could *he* do ?   Then they
sent for a watchmaker, and after a good deal of talking and
investigation, the bird was put into something like order ; but the
watchmaker said that the bird must be carefully treated, for the
barrels were worn, and it would be impossible to put new ones in
in such a manner that the music would go.   There was a great
lamentation ; only once in a year was it permitted to let the bird
sing, and that was almost too much.   But then the playmaster
made a little speech, full of hard words, and said this was just as
good as before—and so of course it was as good as before.

Now five years had gone by, and a real grief came upon the
whole nation.   The Chinese were really fond of their Emperor,
and now he was ill, and could not, it was said, live much longer.
Already a new Emperor had been chosen, and the people stood
out in the street and asked the cavalier how their old Emperor did.

"P !" said he, and shook his head.

Cold and pale lay the Emperor in his great gorgeous bed ; the
whole court thought him dead, and each one ran to pay homage
to the new ruler.   The chamberlains ran out to talk it over, and
the ladies'-maids had a great coffee party.   All about, in all the
halls and passages, cloth had been laid down so that no footstep
could be heard, and therefore it was quiet there, quite quiet.
But the Emperor was not dead yet ; stiff and pale he lay on the
gorgeous bed with the long velvet curtains and the heavy gold
tassels ; high up, a window stood open, and the moon shone in
upon the Emperor and the artificial bird.

The poor Emperor could scarcely breathe ; it was just as if
something lay upon his chest : he opened his eyes, and then he
saw that it was Death who sat upon his chest, and had put on his
golden crown, and held in one hand the Emperor's sword, and in
the other his beautiful banner.   And all around, from among the
folds of the splendid velvet curtains, strange heads peered forth ;

47

a few very ugly, the rest quite lovely and mild.   These were all the Emperor's bad and good deeds, that looked upon him now that Death sat upon his heart.

"Do you remember this?" whispered one after the other, "Do you remember that?" and then they told him so much that the perspiration ran from his forehead.

"I did not know that!" said the Emperor.   "Music! music! the great Chinese drum!" he cried, "so that I need not hear all they say!"

And they continued speaking, and Death nodded like a Chinaman to all they said.

"Music! music!" cried the Emperor.   "You little precious golden bird, sing, sing!   I have given you gold and costly presents; I have even hung my golden slipper around your neck —sing now, sing!"

But the bird stood still; no one was there to wind him up, and he could not sing without that; but Death continued to stare at the Emperor with his great hollow eyes, and it was quiet, fearfully quiet.

Then there sounded from the window, suddenly, the most lovely song.   It was the little live Nightingale, that sat outside on a spray.   It had heard of the Emperor's sad plight, and had come to sing to him of comfort and hope.   And as it sang the spectres grew paler and paler; the blood ran quicker and more quickly through the Emperor's weak limbs; and even Death listened, and said,

"Go on, little Nightingale, go on!"

"But will you give me that splendid golden sword?   Will you give me that rich banner?   Will you give me the Emperor's Crown?"

And Death gave up each of these treasures for a song.   And the Nightingale sang on and on; and it sang of the quiet churchyard where the white roses grow, where the elder-blossom smells sweet, and where the fresh grass is moistened by the tears of survivors. Then Death felt a longing to see his garden, and floated out at the window in the form of a cold white mist.

"Thanks! thanks!" said the Emperor. "You heavenly little bird! I know you well. I banished you from my country and empire, and yet you have charmed away the evil faces from my couch, and banished Death from my heart! How can I reward you?"

"You have rewarded me!" replied the Nightingale. "I have drawn tears from your eyes, when I sang the first time—I shall never forget that. Those are the jewels that rejoice a singer's heart. But now sleep and grow fresh and strong again. I will sing you something."

And it sang, and the Emperor fell into a sweet slumber. Ah! how mild and refreshing that sleep was! The sun shone upon him through the windows, when he awoke refreshed and restored: not one of his servants had yet returned, for they all thought he was dead; only the Nightingale still sat beside him and sang.

"You must always stay with me," said the Emperor. "You shall sing as you please; and I'll break the artificial bird into a thousand pieces."

"Not so," replied the Nightingale. "It did well as long as it could; keep it as you have done till now. I cannot build my nest in the palace to dwell in it, but let me come when I feel the wish; then I will sit in the evening on the spray yonder by the window, and sing you something, so that you may be glad and thoughtful at once. I will sing of those who are happy and of those who suffer. I will sing of the good and the evil that remains hidden round about you. The little singing bird flies far around, to the poor fisherman, to the peasant's roof, to every one who dwells far away from you and from your court. I love your

49

THE NIGHTINGALE

heart more than your crown, and yet the crown has an air of sanctity about it. I will come and sing to you—but one thing you must promise me."

" Everything ! " said the Emperor ; and he stood there in his imperial robes, which he had put on himself, and pressed the sword which was heavy with gold to his heart.

" One thing I beg of you : tell no one that you have a little bird who tells you everything. Then it will go all the better."

And the Nightingale flew away.

The servants came in to look at their dead Emperor, and—yes, there they stood, and the Emperor said " Good morning ! "

OLE · LUK - OIE

HERE'S nobody in the whole world who knows so many stories as Ole Luk-Oie. He can tell capital histories.

Well on in the evening, when the children still sit nicely at table, or upon their stools, Ole Luk-Oie comes. He comes up the stairs quite softly, for he walks in his socks : he opens the door noiselessly, and *whisk !* he squirts sweet milk in the children's eyes, a small, small stream, but enough to prevent them from keeping their eyes open; and thus they cannot see him. He creeps just among them, and blows softly upon their necks, and this makes their heads heavy. Yes, but it doesn't hurt them, for Ole Luk-Oie is very fond of the children ; he only wants them to be quiet, and *that* they are not until they are taken to bed : they are to be quiet that he may tell them stories.

When the children sleep, Ole Luk-Oie sits down upon their bed. He is well dressed : his coat is of silk, but it is impossible to say of what colour, for it shines red, green, and blue, according as he turns. Under each arm he carries an umbrella : the one with pictures on it he spreads over the good children, and then they dream all night the most glorious stories ; but on his other umbrella nothing at all is painted : this he spreads over the naughty children, and these sleep in a dull way, and when they awake in the morning they have not dreamed of anything.

55

OLE LUK-OIE

Now we shall hear how Ole Luk-Oie, every evening through one whole week, came to a little boy named Hjalmar, and what he told him.   There are seven stories, for there are seven days in the week.

MONDAY

" Listen," said Ole Luk-Oie in the evening, when he had put Hjalmar to bed ; " now I'll decorate."

And all the flowers in the flower-pots became great trees, stretching out their long branches under the ceiling of the room and along the walls, so that the whole room looked like a beauteous bower ; and all the twigs were covered with flowers, and each flower was more beautiful than a rose, and smelt so sweet that one wanted to eat it—it was sweeter than jam.   The fruit gleamed like gold, and there were cakes bursting with raisins.   It was incomparably beautiful.   But at the same time a terrible wail sounded from the table drawer, where Hjalmar's school-book lay.

" Whatever can that be ? " said Ole Luk-Oie ; and he went to the table, and opened the drawer.   It was the slate which was suffering from convulsions, for a wrong number had got into the sum, so that it was nearly falling in pieces ; the slate pencil tugged and jumped at its string, as if it had been a little dog who wanted to help the sum ; but he could not.   And thus there was a great lamentation in Hjalmar's copy-book ;   it was quite terrible to hear. On each page the great letters stood in a row, one underneath the other, and each with a little one at its side ; that was the copy ; and next to these were a few more letters which thought they looked just like the first ; and these Hjalmar had written ; but they lay down just as if they had tumbled over the pencil lines on which they were to stand.

" See, this is how you should hold yourself," said the Copy. " Look, sloping in this way, with a powerful swing ! "

56

" Oh, we should be very glad to do that," replied Hjalmar's Letters, " but we cannot ; we are too weakly."

" Then you must take medicine," said Ole Luk-Oie.

" Oh, no," cried they ; and they immediately stood up so gracefully that it was beautiful to behold.

" Yes, now we cannot tell any stories," said Ole Luk-Oie ; "now I must exercise them. One, two ! one, two !" and thus he exercised the Letters ; and they stood quite slender, and as beautiful as any copy can be. But when Ole Luk-Oie went away, and Hjalmar looked at them next morning they were as weak and miserable as ever.

TUESDAY

As soon as Hjalmar was in bed, Ole Luk-Oie touched all the furniture in the room with his little magic squirt, and they immediately began to converse together, and each one spoke of itself, with the exception of the spittoon, which stood silent, and was vexed that they should be so vain as to speak only of themselves, and think only of themselves, without any regard for him who stood so modestly in the corner for every one's use.

Over the chest of drawers hung a great picture in a gilt frame— it was a landscape. One saw therein large old trees, flowers in the grass, and a large lake with a river which flowed round about a forest, past many castles, and far out into the wide ocean.

Ole Luk-Oie touched the painting with his magic squirt, and the birds in it began to sing, the branches of the trees stirred, and the clouds began to move across it ; one could see their shadows glide over the landscape.

Now Ole Luk-Oie lifted little Hjalmar up to the frame, and put the boy's feet into the picture, just in the high grass ; and there he stood ; and the sun shone upon him through the branches of the trees. He ran to the water, and seated himself in a little boat which lay there ; it was painted red and white, the sails gleamed like silver, and six swans, each with a gold circlet round its neck and a bright blue star on its forehead, drew the boat past the great wood, where the trees told of robbers and witches, and the flowers told of the graceful little elves, and of what the butterflies had told them.

Gorgeous fishes, with scales like silver and gold, swam after their boat ; sometimes they gave a spring, so that it splashed in the water ; and birds, blue and red, little and great, flew after them in two long rows ; the gnats danced, and the cockchafers said, "Boom ! boom !" They all wanted to follow Hjalmar, and each one had a story to tell.

That *was* a pleasure voyage. Sometimes the forest was thick and dark, sometimes like a glorious garden full of sunlight and flowers ; and there were great palaces of glass and of marble ; on the balconies stood Princesses, and these were all little girls whom Hjalmar knew well—he had already played with them. Each one stretched forth her hand, and held out the prettiest sugar heart which ever a cake-woman could sell ; and Hjalmar took hold of each sugar heart as he passed by, and the Princess held fast, so that each of them got a piece—she the smaller share, and Hjalmar the larger. At each palace little Princes stood sentry. They shouldered golden swords, and caused raisins and tin soldiers to shower down : one could see that they were real Princes. Sometimes Hjalmar sailed through forests, sometimes through great halls or through the midst of a town. He also came to the town where his nurse lived, who had carried him in her arms when he was quite a little boy, and who had always been so kind to him ; and she nodded and beckoned, and sang the pretty verse she had made herself and had sent to Hjalmar.

> I've loved thee, and kissed thee, Hjalmar, dear boy ;
> I've watched thee waking and sleeping ;

58

> May the good Lord guard thee in sorrow, in joy,
> And have thee in His keeping

And all the birds sang too, the flowers danced on their stalks, and the old trees nodded, just as if Ole Luk-Oie had been telling stories to *them*.

WEDNESDAY

How the rain was streaming down without ! Hjalmar could hear it in his sleep ; and when Ole Luk-Oie opened a window, the water stood right up to the window-sill : there was quite a lake outside, and a noble ship lay close by the house.

"If thou wilt sail with me, little Hjalmar," said Ole Luk-Oie, "thou canst voyage to-night to foreign climes, and be back again to-morrow."

And Hjalmar suddenly stood in his Sunday clothes upon the glorious ship, and immediately the weather became fine, and they sailed through the streets, and steered round by the church ; and now everything was one great wild ocean. They sailed on until land was no longer to be seen, and they saw a number of storks, who also came from their home, and were travelling towards the hot countries : these storks flew in a row, one behind the other, and they had already flown far—far ! One of them was so weary that his wings would scarcely carry him farther : he was the very last in the row, and soon remained a great way behind the rest; at last he sank, with outspread wings, deeper and deeper ; he gave a few more strokes with his pinions, but it was of no use ; now he touched the rigging of the ship with his feet, then he glided down from the sail, and—bump !—he stood upon the deck.

Now the cabin boy took him and put him into the hencoop with the Fowls, Ducks, and Turkeys ; the poor Stork stood among them quite embarrassed.

"Just look at the fellow ! " said all the Fowls.

59

And the Turkey-cock swelled himself up as much as ever he could, and asked the Stork who he was ; and the Ducks walked backwards and quacked to each other, " Quackery ! quackery ! "

And the Stork told them of hot Africa, of the pyramids, and of the ostrich, which runs like a wild horse through the desert ; but the Ducks did not understand what he said, and they said to one another,

" We're all of the same opinion, namely, that he's stupid."

" Yes, certainly he's stupid," said the Turkey-cock ; and he gobbled.

Then the stork was quite silent, and thought of his Africa.

" Those are wonderful thin legs of yours," said the Turkey-cock. " Pray, how much do they cost a yard ? "

" Quack ! quack ! quack ! " grinned all the Ducks ; but the Stork pretended not to hear it at all.

" You may just as well laugh too," said the Turkey-cock to him, " for that was very wittily said. Or was it, perhaps, too high for you ? Yes, yes, he isn't very penetrating. Let us continue to be interesting among ourselves."

And the Hens clucked, and the Ducks quacked, " Gick ! gack ! gick ! gack ! " It was terrible how they made fun among themselves.

But Hjalmar went to the hencoop, opened the back door, and called to the Stork ; and the Stork hopped out to him on to the deck. Now he had rested, and it seemed as if he nodded at Hjalmar, to thank him. Then he spread his wings, and flew away to the warm countries ; but the Fowls clucked, and the Ducks quacked, and the Turkey-cock became fiery red in the face.

" To-morrow we shall make soup of you," said Hjalmar ; and so saying he awoke, and was lying in his little bed. It was a wonderful journey that Ole Luk-Oie had caused him to take that night.

THURSDAY

" I tell you what," said Ole Luk-Oie, " you must not be frightened. Here you shall see a little mouse," and he held out his hand with the pretty little creature in it. " It has come to invite you to a wedding. There are two little mice here who are going to enter into the marriage state to-night. They live under the floor of your mother's store-closet : that is said to be a charming dwelling-place ! "

" But how can I get through the little mouse-hole in the floor ? " asked Hjalmar.

" Let me manage that," said Ole Luk-Oie. " I will make you small."

And he touched Hjalmar with his magic squirt, and the boy began to shrink and shrink, until he was not so long as a finger.

" Now you may borrow the uniform of a tin soldier : I think it would fit you, and it looks well to wear a uniform when one is in society."

" Yes, certainly," said Hjalmar.

And in a moment he was dressed like the smartest of tin soldiers.

" Will you not be kind enough to take a seat in your mamma's thimble ? " asked the Mouse. " Then I shall have the honour of drawing you."

" Will the young lady really take so much trouble ? " cried Hjalmar.

And thus they drove to the mouse's wedding. First they came into a long passage beneath the boards, which was only just so high that they could drive through it in the thimble ; and the whole passage was lit up with rotten wood.

" Is there not a delicious smell here ? " observed the Mouse. " The entire road has been greased with bacon rinds, and there can be nothing more exquisite."

Now they came into the festive hall. On the right hand stood

61

all the little lady mice ; and they whispered and giggled as if they were making fun of each other ; on the left stood all the gentlemen mice, stroking their whiskers with their fore paws ; and in the centre of the hall the bridegroom and bride might be seen standing in a hollow cheese rind, and kissing each other terribly before all the guests ; for of course they were engaged, and were just about to be married.

More and more strangers kept flocking in. One mouse was nearly treading another to death ; and the happy couple had stationed themselves just in the doorway, so that one could neither come in or go out. Like the passage the room had been greased with bacon rinds, and that was the entire banquet ; but for the dessert a pea was produced, in which a mouse belonging to the family had bitten the name of the betrothed pair—that is to say, the first letter of the name : that was something quite out of the common way.

All the mice said it was a beautiful wedding, and that the entertainment had been very agreeable. And then Hjalmar drove home again : he had really been in grand company ; but he had been obliged to shrink in, to make himself little, and to put on a tin soldier's uniform.

FRIDAY

" It is wonderful how many grown-up people there are who would be glad to have me ! " said Ole Luk-Oie ; " especially those who have done something wrong. ' Good little Ole,' they say to me, ' we cannot close our eyes, and so we lie all night and see our evil deeds, which sit on the bedstead like ugly little goblins, and throw hot water over us ; will you not come and drive them away, so that we may have a good sleep ? '—and then they sigh deeply— ' we would really be glad to pay for it. Good night, Ole ; the money lies on the window-sill.' But I do nothing for money," says Ole Luk-Oie.

" What shall we do this evening ? " asked Hjalmar.

" I don't know if you care to go to another wedding to-night. It is of a different kind from that of yesterday. Your sister's great doll, that looks like a man, and is called Hermann, is going to marry the doll Bertha. Moreover, it is the doll's birthday, and, therefore, they will receive very many presents."

" Yes, I know that," replied Hjalmar. " Whenever the dolls want new clothes my sister lets them either keep their birthday or celebrate a wedding ; that has certainly happened a hundred times already."

" Yes, but to-night is the hundred and first wedding ; and when number one hundred and one is past, it is all over ; and that is why it will be so splendid. Only look ! "

And Hjalmar looked at the table. There stood the little cardboard house with the windows illuminated, and in front of it all the tin soldiers were presenting arms. The bride and bridegroom sat quite thoughtful, and with good reason, on the floor, leaning against a leg of the table. And Ole Luk-Oie, dressed up in the grandmother's black gown, married them to each other. When the ceremony was over, all the pieces of furniture struck up the following beautiful song, which the pencil had written for them. It was sung to the melody of the soldiers' tattoo.

> Let the song swell like the rushing wind,
> In honour of those who this day are joined,
> Although they stand here so stiff and blind,
> Because they are both of a leathery kind.
> Hurrah ! hurrah ! though they're deaf and blind,
> Let the song swell like the rushing wind.

And now they received presents—but they had declined to accept provisions of any kind, for they intended to live on love.

" Shall we now go into a summer lodging, or start on a journey ? " asked the bridegroom.

63

And the Swallow, who was a great traveller, and the old yard Hen, who had brought up five broods of chickens, were consulted on the subject. And the Swallow told of the beautiful warm climes, where the grapes hung in ripe heavy clusters, where the air is mild, and the mountains glow with colours unknown here.

" But they have not our green colewort there ! " objected the Hen. " I was in the country, with my children one summer. There was a sand pit, in which we could walk about and scratch ; and we had the *entree* to a garden where green colewort grew : Oh, how green it was ! I cannot imagine anything more beautiful."

" But one cole-plant looks just like another," said the Swallow ; " and the weather here is often so bad."

" One is accustomed to that," said the Hen.

" But it is so cold here, it freezes."

" That is good for the coleworts ! " said the Hen. " Besides, it can also be warm. Did we not, four years ago, have a summer which lasted five weeks ? it was so hot here that one could scarcely breathe ; and then we have not all the poisonous animals that infest these warm countries of yours, and we are free from robbers. He is a villain who does not consider our country the most beautiful— he certainly does not deserve to be here ! " And then the Hen wept, and went on : " I have also travelled. I rode in a coop above fifty miles ; and there is no pleasure at all in travelling ! "

" Yes, the hen is a sensible woman ! " said the doll Bertha. " I don't think anything either of travelling among mountains, for you only have to go up, and then down again. No, we will go into the sand pit beyond the gate, and walk about in the colewort-patch."

And so it was settled.

SATURDAY

" Am I to hear some stories now ? " asked little Hjalmar, as soon as Ole Luk-Oie had got him into bed.

"This evening we have no time for that," replied Ole; and he spread his fine umbrella over the lad, "Only look at these Chinamen!"

And the whole umbrella looked like a great China dish, with blue trees and pointed bridges with little Chinamen upon them, who stood there nodding their heads.

"We must have the whole world prettily decked out for to-morrow morning," said Ole, "for that is a holiday—it is Sunday. I will go to the church steeples to see that the little church goblins are polishing the bells, that they may sound sweetly. I will go out into the field, and see if the breezes are blowing the dust from the grass and leaves; and, what is the greatest work of all, I will bring down all the stars, to polish them. I take them in my apron; but first each one must be numbered, and the holes in which they are fixed up there must be numbered likewise, so that they may be placed in the same holes again; otherwise they would not sit fast, and we should have too many shooting stars, for one after another would fall down."

"Hark-ye! Do you know, Mr. Luk-Oie," said an old Portrait which hung on the wall where Hjalmar slept, "I am Hjalmar's great-grandfather. I thank you for telling the boy stories; but you must not confuse his ideas. The stars cannot be taken down and polished! The stars are world-orbs, just like our own earth, and that is just the good thing about them."

"I thank you, old great-grandfather," said Ole Luk-Oie, "I thank you! You are the head of the family. You are the ancestral head; but I am older than you! I am an old heathen: the Romans and Greeks called me the Dream God. I have been in the noblest houses, and am admitted there still! I know how to act with great people and with small. Now you may tell your own story!" And Ole Luk-Oie took his umbrella, and went away.

"Well, well! May one not even give an opinion now-a-days?"

65

grumbled the old Portrait.   And Hjalmar awoke.

SUNDAY

"Good evening!" said Ole Luk-Oie; and Hjalmar nodded, and ran and turned his great-grandfather's Portrait against the wall, that it might not interrupt them, as it had done yesterday.

"Now you must tell me stories; about the five green peas that lived in one pod, and about the cock's foot that paid court to the hen's foot, and of the darning-needle who gave herself such airs because she thought herself a sewing needle."

"There may be too much of a good thing!" said Ole Luk-Oie. "You know that I prefer showing you something.   I will show you my own brother.   His name, like mine, is Ole Luk-Oie, but he never comes to any one more than once; and he takes him to whom he comes upon his horse, and tells him stories.   He only knows two.   One of these is so exceedingly beautiful that no one in the world can imagine it, and the other so horrible and dreadful that it cannot be described."

And then Ole Luk-Oie lifted little Hjalmar up to the window, and said,

"There you will see my brother the other Ole Luk-Oie.   They also call him Death!   Do you see, he does not look so terrible as they make him in the picture-books, where he is only a skeleton. No, that is silver embroidery that he has on his coat; that is a splended hussar's uniform; a mantle of black velvet flies behind him over the horse.   See how he gallops along!"

And Hjalmar saw how this Ole Luk-Oie rode away, and took young people as well as old upon his horse.   Some of them he put before him, and some behind; but he always asked first, "How stands it with the mark-book?" "Well," they all replied. "Yes, let me see it myself," he said.   And then each one had to show him the book; and those who had "very well" and "remarkably well" written in their books, were placed in front of his horse, and a lovely story was told to them ; while those who had "middling" or "tolerably well" had to sit up behind, and hear a very terrible story indeed. They trembled and wept, and wanted to jump off the horse, but this they could not do, for they had all, as it were, grown fast to it.

"But Death is a most splendid Ole Luk-Oie," said Hjalmar. "I am not afraid of him !"

"Nor need you be," replied Ole Luk-Oie ; "but see that you have a good mark-book !"

"Yes, that is instructive !" muttered the great-grandfather's Picture. "It is of some use after all giving one's opinion." And now he was satisfied.

You see, that is the story of Ole Luk-Oie ; and now he may tell you more himself, this evening !

That *was* a pleasure voyage.   Sometimes the forest was thick and dark, sometimes like a glorious garden full of sunlight and flowers.   *p. 58*

The draught of air caught the dancer, and she flew like a sylph just into
the stove to the tin soldier.   -   -   -   -   -   -   *p.* 77

THE · HARDY · TIN · SOLDIER

HERE were once five and twenty tin soldiers; they were all brothers, for they had all been born of one old tin spoon. They shouldered their muskets, and looked straight before them : their uniform was red and blue, and very splendid. The first thing they had heard in the world, when the lid was taken off their box, had been the words " Tin Soldiers ! " These words were uttered by a little boy, clapping his hands : the soldiers had been given to him, for it was his birthday ; and now he put them upon the table. Each soldier was exactly like the rest only one of them was a little different, he had but one leg, for he had been cast last of all, and there had not been enough tin to finish him ; but he stood as firmly upon his one leg as the others on their two ; and it was just this soldier who became remarkable.

On the table on which they had been placed stood many other playthings, but the toy that attracted most attention was a neat castle of cardboard. Through the little windows one could see straight into the hall. Before the castle some little trees were placed round a little looking-glass, which was to represent a clear lake. Waxen swans swam on this lake and were mirrored in it. This was all very pretty ; but the prettiest of all was a little lady, who stood at the open door of the castle : she was also cut out in paper, but she had a dress of the clearest gauze, and a little narrow

73

THE HARDY TIN SOLDIER

blue ribbon over her shoulders, that looked like a scarf ; and in the middle of this ribbon was a shining tinsel rose as big as her whole face. The little lady stretched out both her arms, for she was a dancer ; and then she lifted one leg so high that the tin soldier could not see it at all, and thought that, like himself, she had but one leg.

" That would be the wife for me," thought he ; "but she is very grand. She lives in a castle, and I have only a box, and there are five and twenty of us in that. It is no place for her. But I must try to make acquaintance with her."

And then he lay down at full length behind a snuff-box which was on the table ; there he could easily watch the little dainty lady, who continued to stand on one leg without losing her balance.

When the evening came, all the other tin soldiers were put into their box, and the people in the house went to bed. Now the toys began to play at " visiting," and at " war " and " giving balls." The tin soldiers rattled in their box, for they wanted to join, but could not lift the lid. The nutcracker threw somersaults, and the pencil amused itself on the table : there was so much noise that the canary woke up, and began to speak too, and even in verse. The only two who did not stir from their places were the tin soldier and the dancing lady : she stood straight up on the point of one of her toes, and stretched out both her arms ; and he was just as enduring on his one leg ; and he never turned his eyes away from her.

Now the clock struck twelve—and, bounce !—the lid flew off the snuff-box ; but there was not snuff in it, but a little black goblin : you see it was a trick.

" Tin soldier ! " said the goblin, " will you keep your eyes to yourself ? "

But the tin soldier pretended not to hear him.

" Just you wait until to-morrow ! " said the goblin.

But when morning came, and the children got up, the tin soldier was placed in the window ; and whether it was the goblin or the draught that did it, all at once the window flew open, and the soldier fell head over heels out of the third story. That was a terrible passage ! He put his leg straight up, and stuck with his helmet downwards and his bayonet between the paving-stones.

The servant-maid and the little boy came down directly to look for him, but though they almost trod upon him they could not see him. If the soldier had cried out " Here I am ! " they would have found him ; but he did not think it fitting to call out loudly because he was in uniform.

Now it began to rain ; the drops soon fell thicker, and at last it came down in a complete stream. When the rain was past, two street boys came by.

" Just look ! " said one of them, " there lies a tin soldier. He shall go out sailing."

And they made a boat out of a newspaper, and put the tin soldier in the middle of it ; and so he sailed down the gutter, and the two boys ran beside him and clapped their hands. Goodness preserve us ! how the waves rose in that gutter, and how fast the stream ran ! But then it had been a heavy rain. The paper boat rocked up and down, and sometimes turned round so rapidly that the tin soldier trembled ; but he remained firm, and never changed countenance, but looked straight before him, and shouldered his musket.

All at once the boat went into a long drain, and it became as dark as if he had been in his box.

" Where am I going now ? " he thought. " Yes, yes, that's the goblin's fault. Ah ! if the little lady only sat here with me in the boat, it might be twice as dark for what I should care."

Suddenly there came a great water-rat, which lived under the drain.

" Have you a passport ? " said the rat. " Give me your passport."

But the tin soldier kept silence, and held his musket tighter than ever.

The boat went on, but the rat came after it. Ugh ! how he gnashed his teeth, and called out to the bits of straw and wood.

" Hold him ! hold him ! he hasn't paid toll—he hasn't shown his passport ! "

But the stream became stronger and stronger. The tin soldier could see the bright daylight where the arch ended ; but he heard a roaring noise, which might well frighten a bolder man. Only think—just where the tunnel ended, the drain ran into a great canal ; and for him that would have been as dangerous as for us to be carried down a great waterfall.

Now he was already so near it that he could not stop. The boat was carried out, the poor tin soldier stiffening himself as much as he could, and no one could say that he moved an eyelid. The boat whirled round three or four times, and was full of water to the very edge—it must sink. The tin soldier stood up to his neck in water, and the boat sank deeper and deeper, and the paper was loosened more and more ; and now the water closed over the soldier's head. Then he thought of the pretty little dancer, and how he should never see her again ; and it sounded in the soldier's ears :

Farewell, farewell, thou warrior brave,
For this day thou must die !

And now the paper parted, and the tin soldier fell out ; but at that moment he was snapped up by a great fish.

Oh, how dark it was in that fish's body ! It was darker yet than in the drain tunnel ; and then it was very narrow too. But the tin soldier remained unmoved, and lay at full length shouldering his musket.

The fish swam to and fro ; he made the most wonderful movements, and then became quite still. At last something flashed through him like lightning. The daylight shone quite clear, and a voice said aloud, " The tin soldier ! " The fish had been caught, carried to market, bought, and taken into the kitchen, where the cook cut him open with a large knife. She seized the soldier round the body with both her hands, and carried him into the room, where all were anxious to see the remarkable man who had travelled about in the inside of a fish ; but the tin soldier was not at all proud. They placed him on the table, and there—no ! What curious things may happen in the world ! The tin soldier was in the very room in which he had been before ! he saw the same children, and the same toys stood on the table ; and there was the pretty castle with the graceful little dancer. She was still balancing herself on one leg, and held the other extended in the air. She was hardy too. That moved the tin soldier : he was very nearly weeping tin tears, but that would not have been proper. He looked at her and she at him, but they said nothing to each other.

Then one of the little boys took the tin soldier and flung him into the stove. He gave no reason for doing this. It must have been the fault of the goblin in the snuff-box.

The tin soldier stood there quite illuminated, and felt a heat that was terrible ; but whether this heat proceeded from the real fire or from love he did not know. The colours had quite gone off from him ; but whether that had happened on the journey, or had been caused by grief, no one could say. He looked at the little lady, she looked at him and he felt that he was melting ; but he still stood firm, shouldering his musket. Then suddenly the door flew open, and the draught of air caught the dancer, and she flew like a sylph just into the stove to the tin soldier, and flashed up into a flame, and she was gone. Then the tin soldier melted down into a lump, and when the servant-maid took the ashes out next day, she found him in the shape of a little tin heart. But of the dancer nothing remained but the tinsel rose, and that was burned as black as a coal.

THE · FLYING · TRUNK

HERE was once a merchant, who was so rich that he could pave the whole street with silver coins, and almost have enough left for a little lane. But he did not do that; he knew how to employ his money differently. When he spent a shilling he got back a crown, such a clever merchant was he; and this continued till he died.

His son now got all this money; and he lived merrily, going to the masquerade every evening, making kites out of dollar notes, and playing at ducks and drakes on the sea coast with gold pieces instead of pebbles. In this way the money might soon be spent, and indeed it was so. At last he had no more than four shillings left, and no clothes to wear but a pair of slippers and an old dressing-gown. Now his friends did not trouble themselves any more about him, as they could not walk with him in the street; but one of them, who was good-natured, sent him an old trunk, with the remark, " Pack up! " Yes, that was all very well, but he had nothing to pack, therefore he seated himself in the trunk.

That was a wonderful trunk. So soon as any one pressed the lock the trunk could fly. This it now did; *whirr!* away it flew with him through the chimney and over the clouds, farther and farther away. But as often as the bottom of the trunk cracked a little he was in great fear lest it might go to pieces, and then he would have thrown a fine somersault! In that way he came to the land of the Turks. He hid the trunk in a wood under some dry leaves, and then went into the town. He could do that very well, for among the Turks all the people went dressed like himself in dressing-gown and slippers. Then he met a nurse with a little child.

"Here, you Turkish nurse," he began "what kind of a great castle is that close by the town, in which the windows are so high up?"

"There dwells the Sultan's daughter," replied she. "It is prophesied that she will be very unhappy respecting a lover; and therefore nobody may go to her, unless the Sultan and Sultana are there too."

"Thank you!" said the merchant's son; and he went out into the forest, seated himself in his trunk, flew on the roof, and crept through the window into the Princess's room.

She was lying asleep on the sofa, and she was so beautiful that the merchant's son was compelled to kiss her. Then she awoke, and was very much startled; but he said he was a Turkish angel who had come down to her through the air, and that pleased her.

They sat down side by side, and he told her stories about her eyes; he told her they were the most glorious dark lakes, and that thoughts were swimming about in them like mermaids. And he told her about her forehead; that it was a snowy mountain with the most splendid halls and pictures. And he told her about the stork who brings the lovely little children.

Yes, those were fine histories! Then he asked the Princess if she would marry him, and she said "Yes," directly.

"But you must come here on Saturday," said she. "Then the Sultan and the Sultana will be here to tea. They will be very proud that I am to marry a Turkish angel. But take care that you know a very pretty story, for both my parents are very fond

80

indeed of stories. My mother likes them high-flown and moral, but my father likes them merry so that one can laugh."

" Yes, I shall bring no marriage gift but a story," said he ; and so they parted. But the Princess gave him a sabre, the sheath embroidered with gold pieces, and that was very useful to him.

Now he flew away, bought a new dressing-gown, and sat in the forest and made up a story ; it was to be ready by Saturday, and that was not an easy thing.

By the time he had finished it Saturday had come. The Sultan and his wife and all the court were at the Princess's to tea. He was received very graciously.

" Will you tell us a story ? " said the Sultana ; " one that is deep and edifying."

" Yes, but one that we can laugh at," said the Sultan.

" Certainly," he replied; and began. And now listen well.

" There was once a bundle of Matches, and these Matches were particularly proud of their high descent. Their genealogical tree, that is to say, the great fir tree of which each of them was a little splinter, had been a great old tree out in the forest. The Matches now lay between a Tinder-box and an old iron Pot ; and they were telling about the days of their youth ' Yes, when we were upon the green boughs,' they said, ' then we really were upon the green boughs ! Every morning and evening there was diamond tea for us, I mean dew ; we had sunshine all day long whenever the sun shone, and all the little birds had to tell stories. We could see very well that we were rich, for the other trees were only dressed out in summer, while our family had the means to wear green dresses in the winter as well. But then the woodcutter came, like a great revolution, and our family was broken up. The head of the family got an appointment as mainmast in a first-rate ship, which could sail round the world if necessary ; the other branches went to other places, and now we have the office of

THE FLYING TRUNK

kindling a light for the vulgar herd. That's how we grand people came to be in the kitchen."

"My fate was of a different kind," said the iron Pot which stood next to the Matches. "From the beginning ever since I came into the world, there has been a great deal of scouring and cooking done in me. I look after the practical part, and am the first here in the house. My only pleasure is to sit in my place after dinner, very clean and neat, and to carry on a sensible conversation with my comrades. But except the Water Pot, which sometimes is taken down into the courtyard, we always live within our four walls. Our only newsmonger is the Market Basket ; but he speaks very uneasily about the government and the people. Yes, the other day there was an old pot that fell down from fright, and burst. He's liberal, I can tell you !" "Now you're talking too much," the Tinder-Box interrupted, and the Steel struck against the Flint, so that sparks flew out. "Shall we not have a merry evening ?"

"Yes, let us talk about who is the grandest," said the Matches.

"No, I don't like to talk about myself," retorted the Pot. "Let us get up an evening entertainment. I will begin. I will tell a story from real life, something that every one has experienced, so that we can easily imagine the situation, and take pleasure in it. On the Baltic, by the Danish beech-trees——"

"That's a pretty beginning !" cried all the Plates "That will be a story we shall like."

"Yes, there I spent my youth in a quiet family where the furniture was polished, and the floors scoured, and new curtains were put up every fortnight."

"What an interesting way you have of telling a story !" said the Carpet Broom. "One can tell directly that the narrator is a woman. There's something pure runs through it."

"Yes, one feels that," said the Water Pot, and out of delight it gave a little hop, so that there was a splash on the floor.

And the Pot went on telling her story, and the end was as good as the beginning.

All the Plates rattled with joy, and the Carpet Broom brought some green parsley out of the dust hole, and put it like a wreath on the Pot, for he knew that it would vex the others. "If I crown her to-day," it thought, "she will crown me to-morrow."

"Now I'll dance," said the Fire Tongs, and she danced. Preserve us! how that implement could lift up one leg! The old Chair Cushion burst to see it. "Shall I be crowned too?" thought the Tongs; and indeed a wreath was awarded.

"They're only common people, after all!" thought the Matches.

Now the Tea Urn was to sing; but she said she had taken cold, and could not sing unless she felt boiling within. But that was only affectation; she did not want to sing, except when she was in the parlour with the grand people.

In the window sat an old Quill Pen, with which the maid generally wrote; there was nothing remarkable about this pen, except that it had been dipped too deep into the ink, but she was proud of that. "If the Tea Urn won't sing," she said, "she may leave it alone. Outside hangs a nightingale in a cage, and he can sing. He hasn't had any education, but this evening we'll say nothing about that."

"I think it very wrong," said the Tea Kettle—he was the kitchen singer, and half-brother to the Tea Urn—"that that rich and foreign bird should be listened to! Is this patriotic? Let the Market Basket decide."

"I am vexed," said the Market Basket. "No one can imagine how much I am secretly vexed. Is that a proper way of spending the evening? Would it not be more sensible to put the house in order? Let each one go to his own place, and I would arrange the whole game. That would be quite another thing."

"Yes, let us make a disturbance," cried they all. Then the door opened, and the maid came in, and they all stood still; not one stirred. But there was not one pot among them who did not know what he could do, and how grand he was. "Yes, if I had liked," each one thought, "it might have been a very merry evening."

The servant girl took the Matches and lighted the fire with them. Mercy! how they sputtered and burst out into flame! "Now every one can see," thought they, "that we are first. How we shine! what a light!"—and they burned out.

"That was a capital story," said the Sultana. "I feel myself quite carried away to the kitchen, to the Matches. Yes, now thou shalt marry our daughter."

"Yes, certainly," said the Sultan, "thou shalt marry our daughter on Monday."

And they called him *thou*, because he was to belong to the family.

The wedding was decided on, and on the evening before it the whole city was illuminated. Biscuits and cakes were thrown among the people, the street boys stood on their toes, called out "Hurrah!" and whistled on their fingers. It was uncommonly splendid.

"Yes, I shall have to give something as a treat," thought the merchant's son. So he bought rockets and crackers, and every imaginable sort of firework, put them all into his trunk, and flew up into the air.

"Crack!" how they went, and how they went off! All the Turks hopped up with such a start that their slippers flew about their ears; such a meteor they had never yet seen. Now they could understand that it must be a Turkish angel who was going to marry the Princess.

As soon as the merchant's son descended again into the forest with his trunk, he thought, "I will go into the town now, and hear how it all looked." And it was quite natural that he wanted to do so.

What stories people told ! Every one whom he asked about it had seen it in a separate way ; but one and all thought it fine.

" I saw the Turkish angel himself," said one. " He had eyes like glowing stars, and a beard like foaming water."

" He flew in a fiery mantle," said another ; "the most lovely little cherub peeped forth from among the folds."

Yes, they were wonderful things that he heard ; and on the following day he was to be married.

Now he went back to the forest to rest himself in his trunk. But what had become of that ? A spark from the fireworks had set fire to it, and the trunk was burned to ashes. He could fly no more, and could not get to his bride.

She stood all day on the roof waiting ; and most likely she is waiting still. But he wanders through the world telling fairy tales; but they are not so merry as that one he told about the Matches.

And then he went into his kingdom and shut the door in her face, and
put a bar on.   So now she might stand outside and sing—   *p. 96*
Oh, my darling Augustine,
All is lost, all is lost.

THE · SWINEHERD

HERE was once a poor Prince, who had a kingdom which was quite small, but still it was large enough that he could marry upon it, and that is what he wanted to do.

Now, it was certainly somewhat bold of him to say to the Emperor's daughter, " Will you have me ? " But he did venture it for his name was famous far and wide : there were hundreds of Princesses who would have been glad to say yes ; but did *she* say so ? Well, we shall see.

On the grave of the Prince's father there grew a rose bush, a very beautiful rose bush. It bloomed only every fifth year, and even then it bore only a single rose, but what a rose that was ! It was so sweet that whoever smelt at it forgot all sorrow and trouble. And then he had a nightingale, which could sing as if all possible melodies were collected in its little throat. This rose and this nightingale the Princess was to have, and therefore they were put into great silver cases and sent to her.

The Emperor caused the presents to be carried before him into the great hall where the Princess was playing at " visiting " with her maids of honour (they did nothing else), and when she saw the great silver cases with the presents in them, she clapped her hands with joy.

" If it were only a little pussy-cat ! " said she.

But then came out the splendid rose.

" Oh, how pretty it is made ! " said all the court ladies.

" It is more than pretty," said the Emperor. " It is charming."

But the Princess felt it, and then she almost began to cry.

" Fie, papa,! " she said, " it is not artificial, it is a *natural* rose ! "

" Fie," said all the court ladies, " it's a natural one ! "

" Let us first see what is in the other case before we get angry," said the Emperor.   And then the nightingale came out ; it sang so beautifully that they did not at once know what to say against it.

" *Superbe ! charmant !* " said the maids of honour, for they all spoke French, the one worse than the other.

" How that bird reminds me of the late Empress's musical snuff-box," said an old cavalier. " Yes, it is the same tone, the same expression."

" Yes," said the Emperor ; and then he wept like a little child.

" I really hope it is not a natural bird," said the Princess.

" Yes, it is a natural bird," said they who had brought it.

" Then let the bird fly away," said the Princess ; and she would by no means allow the Prince to come.

But the Prince was not at all dismayed. He stained his face brown and black, drew his hat down over his brows, and knocked at the door.

" Good day Emperor," he said : " could I not be employed here in the castle ? "

" Well," replied the Emperor, " but there are so many who want places ; but let me see, I want some one who can keep the pigs, for we have many of them."

So the Prince was appointed the Emperor's swineherd. He received a miserable small room down by the pig-sty, and here he was obliged to stay ; but all day long he sat and worked, and when it was evening he had finished a neat little pot, with bells all round it, and when the pot boiled these bells rang out prettily and played the old melody—

Oh, my darling Augustine,
All is lost, all is lost.

But the cleverest thing about the whole arrangement was, that by holding one's finger in the steam from the pot, one could at once smell what food was being cooked at every hearth in the town. That was quite a different thing from the rose.

Now the Princess came with all her maids of honour, and when she heard the melody she stood still and looked quite pleased; for she, too, could play "Oh, my darling Augustine." It was the only thing she could play, but then she played it with one finger.

"Why, that is what I play!" she cried. "He must be an educated swineherd! Hark-ye: go down and ask the price of the instrument."

So one of the maids of honour had to go down; but first she put on a pair of pattens.

"What do you want for the pot?" inquired the lady.

"I want ten kisses from the Princess," replied the swineherd.

"Heaven preserve us!" exclaimed the maid of honour.

"Well I won't sell it for less," said the swineherd.

"Well, what did he say?" asked the Princess.

"I really can't repeat it, it is so shocking," replied the lady.

"Well, you can whisper it in my ear." And the lady whispered it to her.—"He is very rude," declared the Princess: and she went away. But when she had gone a little way, the bells sounded so prettily—

Oh, my darling Augustine,
All is lost, all is lost.

"Hark-ye," said the Princess: "ask him if he will take ten kisses from my maids of honour."

93

" No, thanks," replied the swineherd : " ten kisses from the Princess, or I shall keep my pot."

" How tiresome that is ! " cried the Princess. " But at least you must stand round me, so that nobody sees it."

And the maids of honour stood round her, and spread out their dresses, and then the swineherd received ten kisses, and she received the pot.

Then there was rejoicing ! All the evening and all the day long the pot was kept boiling ; there was not a kitchen hearth in the whole town of which they did not know what it had cooked, at the shoemaker's as well as the chamberlain's. The ladies danced with pleasure, and clapped their hands.

" We know who will have sweet soup and pancakes for dinner, and who has hasty pudding and cutlets ; how interesting that is ! "

" Very interesting ! " said the head lady-superintendent.

" Yes, but keep counsel, for I'm the Emperor's daughter."

" Yes, certainly," said all.

The swineherd, that is to say, the Prince—but of course they did not know but that he was a real swineherd—let no day pass by without doing something, and so he made a rattle ; when any person swung this rattle, he could play all the waltzes, hops, and polkas that have been known since the creation of the world.

" But that is *superbe !* " cried the Princess, as she went past. " I have never heard a finer composition. Hark-ye : go down and ask what the instrument costs ; but I give no more kisses."

" He demands a hundred kisses from the Princess," said the maid of honour who had gone down to make the inquiry.

" I think he must be mad ! " exclaimed the Princess ; and she went away ; but when she had gone a little distance she stood still. " One must encourage art," she observed. " I am the Emperor's daughter ! Tell him he shall receive ten kisses, like last time, and he may take the rest from my maids of honour."

" Ah, but we don't like to do it ! " said the maids of honour.

" That's all nonsense ! " retorted the Princess, "and if I can allow myself to be kissed, you can too ; remember, I give you board and wages."

And so the maids of honour had to go down to him again.

" A hundred kisses from the Princess," said he " or each shall keep his own."

" Stand round me," said she then ; and all the maids of honour stood round her while he kissed the Princess.

" What is that crowd down by the pig-sty ? " asked the Emperor, who had stepped out to the balcony. He rubbed his eyes and put on his spectacles. " Why, those are the maids of honour, at their tricks, yonder ; I shall have to go down to them."

And he pulled up his slippers behind, for they were shoes that he had trodden down at heel. Gracious mercy, how he hurried ! So soon as he came down in the courtyard, he went quite softly, and the maids of honour were too busy counting the kisses, and seeing fair play, to notice the Emperor. Then he stood on tip-toe.

" What's that ? " said he, when he saw that there was kissing going on ; and he hit them on the head with his slipper, just as the swineherd was taking the eighty-sixth kiss.

" Be off ! " said the Emperor, for he was angry.

And the Princess and the swineherd were both expelled from his dominions. So there she stood and cried, the rain streamed down, and the swineherd scolded.

" Oh, miserable wretch that I am ! " said the Princess ; " if I had only taken the handsome Prince ! Oh, how unhappy I am ! "

Then the swineherd went behind a tree, washed the stains from his face, threw away the shabby clothes, and stepped forth in his princely attire, so handsome that the Princess was fain to bow before him.

" I have come to this, that I despise you," said he. " You would not have an honest Prince ; you did not value the rose and the nightingale, but for a plaything you kissed the swineherd, and now you have your reward."

And then he went into his kingdom and shut the door in her face, and put a bar on. So now she might stand outside and sing—

> Oh, my darling Augustine,
> All is lost, all is lost.

THE · SHEPHERDESS · AND · THE · CHIMNEY · SWEEP

AVE you ever seen a very old wooden cupboard, quite black with age, and ornamented with carved foliage and arabesques. Just such a cupboard stood in a parlour : it had been a legacy from the great-grandmother, and was covered from top to bottom with carved roses and tulips. There were the quaintest flourishes upon it, and from among these peered forth little stags' heads with antlers. In the middle of the cupboard door an entire figure of a man had been cut out : he was certainly ridiculous to look at, and he grinned, for you could not call it laughing : he had goat's legs, little horns on his head, and a long beard. The children in the room always called him the Billygoat-legs-Lieutenant-and-Major-General-War-Commander-Sergeant ; that was a difficult name to pronounce, and there are not many who obtain this title ; but it was something to have cut him out. And there he was ! He was always looking at the table under the mirror, for on this table stood a lovely little Shepherdess made of china. Her shoes were gilt, her dress was neatly caught up with a red rose, and besides this she had a golden hat and a shepherd's crook she was very lovely. Close by her stood a little Chimney-Sweeper, black as a coal, but also made of porcelain : he was as clean and neat as any other man, for it was only make-believe that he was a sweep ; the china-workers might just as well have made a prince of him, if they had been so minded.

There he stood very nattily with his ladder, and with a face as white and pink as a girl's ; and that was really a fault, for he ought to have been a little black. He stood quite close to the Shepherdess ; they had both been placed where they stood ; but as they had been placed there they had become engaged to each other. They suited each other well. Both were young people, both made of the same kind of china, and both equally frail.

Close to them stood another figure, three times greater than they. This was an old Chinaman, who could nod. He was also of porcelain, and declared himself to be the grandfather of the little Shepherdess ; but he could not prove his relationship. He declared he had authority over her, and that, therefore, he had nodded to Mr. Billygoat-legs-Lieutenant-and-Major-General-War-Commander-Sergeant, who was wooing her for his wife.

" Then you will get a husband ! " said the old Chinaman, " a man who I verily believe is made of mahogany. He can make you a Billygoat-legs-Lieutenant-and-Major-General-War-Commander-Sergeantess ; he has the whole cupboard full of silver plate, besides what he hoards up in secret drawers."

" I won't go into the dark cupboard ! " said the little Shepherdess. " I have heard tell that he has eleven porcelain wives in there."

" Then you may become the twelfth," cried the Chinaman. " This night, so soon as it creaks in the old cupboard, you shall be married, as true as I am an old Chinaman ! "

And with that he nodded his head and fell asleep. But the little Shepherdess wept and looked at her heart's beloved, the porcelain Chimney-Sweeper.

" I should like to beg of you," said she, " to go out with me into the wide world, for we cannot remain here."

" I'll do whatever you like," replied the little Chimney-Sweeper.

" Let us start directly !   I think I can keep you by exercising my profession."

" If we were only safely down from the table ! " said she. " I shall not be happy until we are out in the wide world."

And he comforted her, and showed her how she must place her little foot upon the carved corners and the gilded foliage down the leg of the table ; he brought his ladder, too, to help her, and they were soon together upon the floor.   But when they looked up at the old cupboard there was great commotion within : all the carved stags were stretching out their heads, rearing up their antlers, and turning their necks ; and the Billygoat-legs-Lieutenant-and-Major-General-War-Commander-Sergeant sprang high in the air, and called across to the old Chinaman.

" Now they're running away ! now they're running away ! "

Then they were a little frightened, and jumped quickly into the drawer of the window-seat.   Here were three or four packs of cards which were not complete, and a little puppet-show, which had been built up as well as it could be done.   There plays were acted, and all the ladies, diamonds, clubs, hearts, and spades, sat in the first row, fanning themselves with their tulips ; and behind them stood all the knaves, showing that they had a head above and below, as is usual in playing-cards.   The play was about two people who were not to be married to each other, and the Shepherdess wept, because it was just like her own history.

" I cannot bear this ! " said she.   " I must go out of the drawer."

But when they arrived on the floor, and looked up at the table, the old Chinaman was awake and was shaking over his whole body—for below he was all one lump.

" Now the old Chinaman's coming ! " cried the little Shepherdess ; and she fell down upon her porcelain knee, so startled was she.

" I have an idea," said the Chimney-Sweeper.   " Shall we

creep into the great *pot-pourri* vase which stands in the corner ? Then we can lie on roses and lavender, and throw salt in his eyes if he comes."

" That will be of no use," she replied. " Besides, I know that the old Chinaman and the *pot-pourri* vase were once engaged to each other, and a kind of liking always remains when people have stood in such a relation to each other. No, there's nothing left for us but to go out into the wide world."

" Have you really courage to go in the wide world with me ? " asked the Chimney-Sweeper. " Have you considered how wide the world is, and that we can never come back here again ? "

" I have," replied she.

And the Chimney-Sweeper looked fondly at her, and said,

" My way is through the chimney. If you have really courage to creep with me through the stove—through the iron fire-box as well as up the pipe, then we can get out into the chimney, and I know how to find my way through there. We'll mount so high that they can't catch us, and quite at the top there's a hole that leads out into the wide world."

And he led her to the door of the stove.

" It looks very black there," said she ; but still she went with him, through the box and through the pipe, where it was pitch-dark night.

" Now we are in the chimney," said he ; " and look, look ! up yonder a beautiful star is shining."

And it was a real star in the sky, which shone straight down upon them, as if it would show them the way. And they clambered and crept : it was a frightful way, and terribly steep ; but he supported her and helped her up ; he held her, and showed her the best places where she could place her little porcelain feet ; and thus they reached the edge of the chimney, and upon that they sat down, for they were desperately tired, as they well might be.

THE SHEPHERDESS AND THE CHIMNEY-SWEEPER

The sky with all its stars was high above, and all the roofs of the town deep below them. They looked far around—far, far out into the world. The poor Shepherdess had never thought of it as it really was : she leaned her little head against the Chimney-Sweeper, then she wept so bitterly that the gold ran down off her girdle.

"That is too much," she said. "I cannot bear that. The world is too large ! If I were only back upon the table below the mirror ! I shall never be happy until I am there again. Now I have followed you out into the wide world, you may accompany me back again if you really love me."

And the Chimney-Sweeper spoke sensibly to her—spoke of the old Chinaman and of the Billygoat-legs-Lieutenant-and-Major-General-War-Commander-Sergeant ; but she sobbed bitterly and kissed her little Chimney-Sweeper, so that he could not help giving way to her, though it was foolish.

And so with much labour they climbed down the chimney again. And they crept through the pipe and the fire-box. That was not pleasant at all. And there they stood in the dark stove ; there they listened behind the door, to find out what was going on in the room. Then it was quite quiet : they look in—ah ! there lay the old Chinaman in the middle of the floor ! He had fallen down from the table as he was pursuing them, and now he lay broken into three pieces ; his back had come off all in one piece, and his head had rolled into a corner. The Billygoat-legs-Lieutenant-and-Major-General-War-Commander-Sergeant stood where he had always stood, considering.

"That is terrible !" said the little Shepherdess. "The old grandfather has fallen to pieces, and it is our fault. I shall never survive it !" And then she wrung her little hands. "He can be mended ! he can be mended !" said the Chimney-Sweeper. "Don't be so violent. If they glue his back together and give him a good rivet in his neck he will be as good as new, and may say many a disagreeable thing to us yet."

" Do you think so ? " cried she.

So they climbed back upon the table where they used to stand.

" You see, we have come back to this," said the Chimney-Sweeper : " we might have saved ourselves all the trouble we have had."

" If the old grandfather were only riveted !" said the Shepherdess. " I wonder if that is dear ? "

And he was really riveted. The family had his back cemented, and a great rivet was passed through his neck : he was as good as new, only he could no longer nod.

" It seems you have become proud since you fell to pieces," said the Billygoat-legs-Lieutenant-and-Major-General-War-Com-mander-Sergeant. " I don't think you have any reason to give yourself such airs. Am I to have her, or am I not ? "

And the Chimney-Sweeper and the little Shepherdess looked at the old Chinaman most piteously, for they were afraid he might nod. But he could not do that, and it was irksome to him to tell a stranger that he always had a rivet in his neck. And so the porcelain people remained together, and they blessed Grandfather's rivet, and loved one another until they broke.

" We'll mount so high that they can't catch us, and quite at the top there's a hole that leads out into the wide world." - - *p.* 102

MOTHER sat by her little child : she was very sorrowful, fearing that it would die. Its little face was pale, and its eyes were closed. The child drew its breath with difficulty, and sometimes as deeply as if it were sighing; and then the mother looked more sorrowfully than before on the little creature.

There was a knock at the door, and a poor old man came in, wrapped up in something that looked like a great horse-cloth, for that keeps one warm ; and he needed it, for it was cold winter. Without, everything was covered with ice and snow, and the wild wind blew so sharply that it cut one's face.

And as the old man trembled with cold, and the child was quiet for a moment, the mother went and put some beer on the stove in a little pot, to warm it for him. The old man sat down and rocked the cradle, and the mother seated herself on a chair by him, looked at her sick child that drew its breath so painfully, and lifted the little hand.

"You think I shall keep it, do you not?" she asked. "The good God will not take it from me!"

And the old man—he was *Death*—nodded in such a strange way, that it might just as well mean *yes* as *no*. And the mother cast down her eyes, and tears rolled down her cheeks. Her head became heavy : for three days and three nights she had not closed

And death went away with her child into the unknown land. - *p.* 114

107

her eyes ; and now she slept, but only for a minute ; then she started up and shivered with cold.

" What is that ? " she asked, and looked round on all sides ; but the old man was gone, and her little child was gone ; he had taken it with him. And there in the corner the old clock was humming and whirring ; the heavy leaden weight ran down to the floor— plump !—and the clock stopped.

But the poor mother rushed out of the house crying for her child.

Out in the snow sat a woman in long black garments, and she said, " Death has been with you in your room ; I saw him hasten away with your child : he strides faster than the wind, and never brings back what he has taken away."

" Only tell me which way he has gone," said the mother. " Tell me the way, and I will find him."

" I know him," said the woman in the black garments ; " but before I tell you, you must sing me all the songs that you have sung to your child. I love those songs ; I have heard them before. I am Night, and I saw your tears when you sang them."

" I will sing them all, all ! " said the mother. " But do not detain me, that I may overtake him, and find my child."

But Night sat dumb and still. Then the mother wrung her hands, and sang and wept. And there were many songs, but yet more tears, and then Night said, " Go to the right into the dark fir wood ; for I saw Death take that path with your little child."

Deep into the forest there was a cross-road, and she did not know which way to take. There stood a thorn bush, with not a leaf nor a blossom upon it ; for it was in the cold winter-time, and icicles hung from the twigs.

" Have you not seen Death go by, with my little child ? "

" Yes," replied the Bush, " but I shall not tell you which way he went unless you warm me in your bosom. I'm freezing to death here, I'm turning to ice."

And she pressed the thorn bush to her bosom, quite close, that it might be well warmed. And the thorns pierced into her flesh, and her blood oozed out in great drops. But the thorn shot out fresh green leaves, and blossomed in the dark winter night : so warm is the heart of a sorrowing mother ! And the thorn bush told her the way that she should go.

Then she came to a great lake, on which there were neither ships nor boat. The lake was not frozen enough to carry her, nor sufficiently open to allow her to wade through, and yet she must cross it if she was to find her child. Then she laid herself down to drink the lake ; and that was impossible for any one to do. But the sorrowing mother thought that perhaps a miracle might be wrought.

"No, that can never succeed," said the lake. "Let us rather see how we can agree. I'm fond of collecting pearls, and your eyes are the two clearest I have ever seen : if you will weep them out into me I will carry you over into the great greenhouse, where Death lives and cultivates flowers and trees ; each of these is a human life."

"Oh, what would I not give to get my child !" said the afflicted mother ; and she wept yet more, and her eyes fell into the depths of the lake, and became two costly pearls. But the lake lifted her up, as if she sat in a swing, and was wafted to the opposite shore, where stood a wonderful house, miles in length. One could not tell if it was a mountain containing forests and caves, or a place that had been built. But the poor mother could not see it, for she had wept her eyes out.

"Where shall I find Death, who went away with my little child ?" she asked.

"He has not arrived here yet," said the old grave-woman, who was going about and watching the hothouse of Death. "How have you found your way here, and who helped you."

"The good God has helped me," she replied. "He is merciful, and you will be merciful too. Where shall I find my little child?"

"I do not know it," said the old woman, "and you cannot see. Many flowers and trees have faded this night, and death will soon come and transplant them. You know very well that every human being has his tree of life, or his flower of life, just as each is arranged. They look like other plants, but their hearts beat. Children's hearts can beat too. Go by that. Perhaps you may recognize the beating of your child's heart. But what will you give me if I tell you what more you must do?"

"I have nothing more to give," said the afflicted mother. "But I will go for you to the ends of the earth."

"I have nothing for you to do there," said the old woman, "but you can give me your long black hair. You must know yourself that it is beautiful, and it pleases me. You can take my white hair for it, and that is always something."

"If you ask for nothing more," said she, "I will give you that gladly." And she gave her beautiful hair and received in exchange the old woman's white hair.

And then they went into the great hothouse of death, where flowers and trees were growing marvellously together. There stood the fine hyacinths under glass bells, and there stood large, sturdy peonies; there grew water-plants, some quite fresh, others somewhat sickly; water-snakes were twining about them, and black crabs clung tightly to the stalks. There stood gallant palm trees, oaks, and plantains, and parsley and blooming thyme. Each tree and flower had its name; each was a human life: the people were still alive, one in China, another in Greenland, scattered about in the world. There were great trees thrust into little pots, so that they stood quite crowded, and were nearly bursting the pots; there was also many a little weakly flower in rich earth, with moss round about it, cared for and tended. But the sorrowful mother bent down over all the smallest plants, and heard the human heart beating in each, and out of the millions she recognized that of her child.

" That is it ! " she cried, and stretched out her hands over a little blue crocus flower, which hung down quite sick and pale.

" Do not touch the flower," said the old dame ; " but place yourself here ; and when Death comes—I expect him every minute—then don't let him pull up the plant, but threaten him that you will do the same to the other plants ; then he'll be frightened. He has to account for them all ; not one may be pulled up till he receives commission from Heaven."

And all at once there was an icy cold rush through the hall, and the blind mother felt that death was arriving.

" How did you find your way hither ? " said he. " How have you been able to come quicker than I ? "

" I am a mother," she answered.

And Death stretched out his long hands towards the little delicate flower ; but she kept her hands tight about it, and held it fast ; and yet she was full of anxious care lest she should touch one of the leaves. Then Death breathed upon her hands, and she felt that his breath was colder than the icy wind ; and her hands sank down powerless.

" You can do nothing against me," said Death.

" But the merciful God can," she replied.

" I only do what He commands," said Death. " I am His gardener. I take all His trees and flowers, and transplant them into the great Paradise gardens, in the unknown land. But how they will flourish there, and how it is there, I may not tell you."

" Give me back my child," said the mother ; and she implored and wept. All at once she grasped two pretty flowers with her two hands, and called to Death, " I'll tear off all your flowers, for I am in despair."

" Do not touch them," said Death. " You say you are so

unhappy, and now you would make another mother just as unhappy!"

"Another mother?" said the poor woman; and she let the flowers go.

"There are your eyes for you," said Death. "I have fished them up out of the lake; they gleamed up quite brightly. I did not know that they were yours. Take them back—they are clearer now than before—and then look down into the deep well close by. I will tell you the names of the two flowers you wanted to pull up, and you will see their whole future, their whole human life; you will see what you were about to frustrate and destroy."

And she looked down into the well, and it was a happiness to see how one of them became a blessing to the world, how much joy and gladness was diffused around her. And the woman looked at the life of the other, and it was made up of care and poverty, misery and woe.

"Both are the will of God," said Death.

"Which of them is the flower of misfortune, and which the blessed one?" she asked.

"That I may not tell you," answered Death; "but this much you shall hear, that one of these two flowers is that of your child. It was the fate of your child that you saw—the future of your own child."

Then the mother screamed aloud for terror.

"Which of them belongs to my child? Tell me that! Release the innocent child! Let my child free from all that misery! Rather carry it away! Carry it into God's kingdom! Forget my tears, forget my entreaties, and all that I have done!"

"I do not understand you," said Death. "Will you have your child back, or shall I carry it to that place that you know not?"

Then the mother wrung her hands, and fell on her knees, and prayed to the good God.

THE STORY OF A MOTHER

"Hear me not when I pray against Thy will, which is at all times the best! Hear me not! Hear me not!" And she let her head sink down on her bosom.

And Death went away with her child into the unknown land.

THE · SNOW · QUEEN

IN SEVEN STORIES

FIRST STORY

WHICH TREATS OF THE MIRROR AND FRAGMENTS

OOK you, now we're going to begin. When we are at the end of the story we shall know more than we do now, for he was a bad goblin. He was one of the very worst, for he was the devil himself. One day he was in very high spirits, for he had made a mirror which had this peculiarity, that everything good and beautiful that was reflected in it shrank together into almost nothing, but that whatever was worthless and looked ugly became prominent and looked worse than ever. The most lovely landscapes seen in this mirror looked like boiled spinach, and the best people became hideous, or stood on their heads and had no stomachs ; their faces were so distorted as to be unrecognizable, and a single freckle was shown spread out over nose and mouth. That was very amusing, the devil said. When a good pious thought passed through any person's mind, there came a grin in the mirror, so that the devil chuckled at his artistic invention. Those who went to the goblin school—for he kept a goblin school—declared everywhere that a wonder had been wrought. For now, they asserted, one could see, for the first time, how the world and the people in it really looked.

THE SNOW QUEEN

They ran about with the mirror, and at last there was not a single country or person that had not been distorted in it. Now they wanted to fly up to heaven, to sneer and scoff at the angels themselves. The higher they flew with the mirror, the more it grinned ; they could scarcely hold it fast. They flew higher and higher, and then the mirror trembled so terribly amid its grinning that it fell down out of their hands to the earth, where it was shattered into a hundred million million and more fragments. And now this mirror, occasioned much more unhappiness than before ; for some of the fragments were scarcely so large as a barleycorn, and these flew about in the world and whenever they flew in any one's eye they stuck there, and those people saw everything wrongly, or had only eyes for the bad side of a thing, for every little fragment of the mirror had retained the same power which the whole glass possessed. A few persons even got a fragment of the mirror into their hearts, and that was terrible indeed, for such a heart became a block of ice. A few fragments of the mirror were so large that they were used as window-panes, but it was a bad thing to look at one's friends through these panes ; other pieces were made into spectacles, and then it went badly when people put on these spectacles to see rightly and to be just ; and the demon laughed till his paunch shook, for it tickled him so. But without, some little fragments of glass still floated about in the air—and now we shall hear.

SECOND STORY

A LITTLE BOY AND A LITTLE GIRL

In the great town, where there are many houses and so many people that there is not room enough for every one to have a little garden, and where, consequently, most persons are compelled to be content with some flowers in flower-pots, were two poor children who possessed a garden somewhat larger than a flower-pot. They were not brother and sister, but they loved each other quite as much as if they had been.   Their parents lived just opposite each other in two garrets, there where the roof on one neighbour's house joined that of another ; and where the water-pipe ran between the two houses was a little window ; one had only to step across the pipe to get from one window to the other.

The parents of each child had a great box, in which grew kitchen herbs that they used, and a little rose bush ; there was one in each box, and they grew famously.   Now it occurred to the parents to place the boxes across the pipe, so that they reached from one window to another, and looked quite like two embankments of flowers.   Pea plants hung down over the boxes, and the rose bushes shot forth long twigs, which clustered round the windows and bent down towards each other : it was almost like a triumphal arch of flowers and leaves.   As the boxes were very high, and the children knew that they might not creep upon them, they often obtained permission to step out upon the roof behind the boxes, and to sit upon their stools under the roses, and there they could play capitally.

In the winter there was an end of this amusement.   The windows were sometimes quite frozen all over.   But then they warmed copper farthings on the stove, and held the warm coins against the frozen pane ; and this made a capital peep-hole so round, so round ! and behind it gleamed a pretty mild eye at each window; and these eyes belonged to the little boy and the little girl.   His name was Kay and the little girl's was Gerda.

In the summer they could get to one another at one bound ; but in the winter they had to go down and up the long staircase, while the snow was pelting without.

"Those are the white bees swarming," said the old grandmother.

"Have they a Queen-bee ? " asked the little boy.   For he knew that there is one among the real bees.

"Yes, they have one," replied grandmamma.   She always flies where they swarm thickest. She is the largest of them all, and never remains quite upon the earth ; she flies up again into the black cloud. Many a midnight she is flying through the streets of the town, and looks in at the windows, and then they freeze in such a strange way, and look like flowers."

"Yes, I've seen that !" cried both the children ; and now they knew that it was true.

"Can the Snow Queen come in here ?" asked the little girl.

"Only let her come," cried the boy ; "I'll set her upon the warm stove, and then she'll melt."

But grandmother smoothed his hair, and told some other tales.

In the evening, when little Kay was at home and half undressed, he clambered upon the chair by the window, and looked through the little hole. A few flakes of snow were falling outside, and one of them, the largest of them all, remained lying on the edge of one of the flower-boxes. The snowflake grew larger and larger, and at last became a maiden clothed in finest white gauze, made out of millions of starry flakes. She was beautiful and delicate, but of ice—of shining, glittering ice. Yet she was alive ; her eyes flashed like two clear stars, but there was no peace or rest in them. She nodded towards the window, and beckoned with her hand. The little boy was frightened, and sprang down from the chair ; then it seemed as if a great bird flew by outside, in front of the window.

Next day there was a clear frost, then there was a thaw, and then the spring came ; the sun shone, the green sprouted forth, the swallows built nests, the windows were opened, and the little children again sat in their garden high up in the roof over all the floors.

How splendidly the roses bloomed this summer ! The little girl had learned a psalm, in which mention was made of roses ; and in speaking of roses, she thought of her own ; and she sang it to

the little boy, and he sang too,—

> The roses in the valleys grow
> Where we the infant Christ shall know.

And the little ones held each other by the hand, kissed the roses, looked at God's bright sunshine, and spoke to it, as if the Christ-child were there. What splendid summer days those were ! How beautiful it was without, among the fresh rose bushes, which seemed as if they would never leave off blooming !

Kay and Gerda sat and looked at the picture-book of beasts and birds. Then it was, while the clock was just striking five on the church tower, that Kay said,

" Oh ! something struck my heart and pricked me in the eye."

The little girl fell upon his neck ; he blinked his eyes. No, there was nothing at all to be seen.

" I think it is gone," said he ; but it was not gone. It was just one of those glass fragments which sprang from the mirror— the magic mirror that we remember well, the ugly glass that made everything great and good which was mirrored in it to seem small and mean, but in which the mean and wicked things were brought out in relief, and every fault was noticeable at once. Poor little Kay had also received a splinter just in his heart, and that will now soon become like a lump of ice. It did not hurt him now, but the splinter was still there.

" Why do you cry ? " he asked. " You look ugly like that. There's nothing the matter with me. Oh, fie ! " he suddenly exclaimed, " that rose is worm-eaten, and this one is quite crooked. After all, they're ugly roses. They're like the box in which they stand."

And then he kicked the box with his foot, and tore both the roses off.

" Kay, what are you about ? " cried the little girl.

And when he noticed her fright he tore off another rose, and

A few persons even got a fragment of the mirror into their hearts, and that was terrible indeed, for such a heart became a block of ice. *p.*118

But Gerda and Kay went hand in hand, and as they went it became beautiful Spring, with green and wild flowers. -   -   -   *p.* 155

then sprang in at his own window, away from pretty little Gerda.

When she afterwards came with her picture-book, he said it was only fit for babies in arms; and when grandmother told stories he always came in with a *but*; and when he could manage it he would get behind her, put on a pair of spectacles, and talk just as she did; he could do that very cleverly, and the people laughed at him. Soon he could mimic the speech and the gait of everybody in the street. Everything that was peculiar or ugly about them Kay could imitate; and people said, "That boy must certainly have a remarkable head." But it was the glass he had got in his eye, the glass that stuck deep in his heart; so it happened that he even teased little Gerda, who loved him with all her heart.

His games now became quite different from what they were before; they became quite sensible. One winter's day when it snowed he came out with a great burning glass, held up the blue tail of his coat, and let the snowflakes fall into it.

"Now look at the glass, Gerda," said he.

And every flake of snow was magnified, and looked like a splendid flower, or a star with ten points: it was beautiful to behold.

"See how clever that is," said Kay. "That's much more interesting than real flowers; and there is not a single fault in it— they're quite regular until they begin to melt."

Soon after Kay came in thick gloves, and with his sledge upon his back. He called up to Gerda "I've got leave to go into the great square, where the other boys play," and he was gone.

In the great square the boldest among the boys often tied their sledges to the country people's carts, and thus rode with them a good way. They went capitally. When they were in the midst of their playing there came a great sledge. It was painted quite white, and in it sat somebody wrapped in a rough white fur, and with a white rough cap on his head. The sledge drove twice round the square, and Kay bound his little sledge to it, and so he drove on with it. It went faster and faster, straight into the next street. The man who drove turned round and nodded in a friendly way to Kay ; it was as if they knew one another : each time when Kay wanted to cast loose his little sledge, the stranger nodded again, and then Kay remained where he was, and thus they drove out at the town gate. Then the snow began to fall so rapidly that the boy could not see a hand's breadth before him, but still he drove on. Now he hastily dropped the cord, so as to get loose from the great sledge, but that was no use, for his sledge was fast bound to the other, and they went on like the wind. Then he called out quite loudly, but nobody heard him ; and the snow beat down, and the sledge flew onward ; every now and then it gave a jump, and they seemed to be flying over hedges and ditches. The boy was quite frightened. He wanted to say his prayers, but could remember nothing but the multiplication table.

The snowflakes became larger and larger ; at last they looked like great white fowls. All at once they sprang aside and the great sledge stopped, and the person who had driven it rose up. The fur and the cap were made altogether of ice. It was *a lady*, tall and slender, and brilliantly white : it was the Snow Queen.

" We have driven well ! " said she. " But why do you tremble with cold ? Creep into my fur."

And she seated him beside her in her own sledge, and wrapped the fur round him, and he felt as if he had sank into a snow-drift.

" Are you still cold ? " asked she, and she kissed him on the forehead.

Oh, that was colder than ice ; it went quite through to his heart, half of which was already a lump of ice : he felt as if he were going to die ; but only for a moment ; for then he seemed quite well, and he did not notice the cold all about him.

" My sledge ! don't forget my sledge."

THE SNOW QUEEN

That was the first thing he thought of; and it was bound fast to one of the white chickens, and this chicken flew behind him with the sledge upon his back. The Snow Queen kissed Kay again, and then he had forgotten little Gerda, his grandmother and all at home.

" Now you shall have no more kisses," said she, " for if you do I should kiss you to death."

Kay looked at her. She was so beautiful, he could not imagine a more sensible or lovely face; she did not appear to him to be made of ice now as before, when she sat at the window and beckoned to him. In his eyes she was perfect; he did not feel at all afraid. He told her that he could do mental arithmetic as far as fractions, that he knew the number of square miles, and the number of inhabitants in the country. And she always smiled and then it seemed to him that what he knew was not enough, and he looked up into the wide sky, and she flew with him high up upon the black cloud, and the storm blew and whistled; it seemed as though the wind sang old songs. They flew over woods and lakes, over sea and land : below them roared the cold wind, the wolves howled, the snow crackled ; over them flew the black screaming crows; but above all the moon shone bright and clear, and Kay looked at the long, long winter night ; by day he slept at the feet of the Queen.

THIRD STORY

The Flower Garden of the Woman who could
Conjure

But how did it fare with little Gerda when Kay did not return? What could have become of him? No one knew, no one could give information. The boys only told that they had seen him bind his sledge to another very large one, which had driven along the street and out at the town gate. Nobody knew what had become of him; many tears were shed, and little Gerda especially wept long and bitterly: then they said he was dead—he had been drowned in the river which flowed close by their town. Oh, those were very dark long winter days! But now spring came, with warmer sunshine.

"Kay is dead and gone," said little Gerda.

"I don't believe it," said the Sunshine.

"He is dead and gone," said she to the Swallows.

"We don't believe it," they replied; and at last little Gerda did not believe it herself.

"I will put on my new red shoes," she said one morning, "those that Kay has never seen; and then I will go down to the river, and ask for him."

It was still very early; she kissed the old grandmother, who was still asleep, put on her red shoes, and went quite alone out of the town gate towards the river.

"Is it true that you have taken away my little playmate from me? I will give you my red shoes if you will give him back to me!"

And it seemed to her as if the waves nodded quite strangely; and then she took her red shoes, that she liked best of anything she possessed, and threw them both into the river; but they fell close to the shore, and the little wavelets carried them back to her, to the land. It seemed as if the river would not take from her the dearest things she possessed because it had not her little Kay; but she thought she had not thrown the shoes far enough out; so she crept into a boat that lay among the reeds; she went to the other end of the boat, and threw the shoes from thence into the water; but the boat was not bound fast, and at the movement she made it glided away from the shore. She noticed it, and hurried to get back, but before she reached the other end the boat was a yard from the bank, and it drifted away faster than before.

Then little Gerda was very much frightened, and began to cry;

but no one heard her except the Sparrows, and they could not carry her to land ; but they flew along by the shore, and sang, as if to console her, " Here we are ! here we are ! " The boat drove on with the stream, and little Gerda sat quite still, with only her stockings on her feet ; her little red shoes floated along behind her, but they could not come up to the boat, for that made more way.

It was very pretty on both shores. There were beautiful flowers, old trees, and slopes with sheep and cows ; but not *one* person was to be seen.

" Perhaps the river will carry me to Kay," thought Gerda.

And then she became more cheerful, and rose up, and for many hours she watched the charming green banks ; then she came to a great cherry orchard, in which stood a little house with remarkable blue and red windows ; it had a thatched roof, and without stood two wooden soldiers, who presented arms to those who sailed past.

Gerda called to them, for she thought they were alive, but of course they did not answer. She came quite close to them ; the river carried the boat towards the shore.

Gerda called still louder, and then there came out of the house an old, old woman leaning on a crutch : she had on a great sun-hat, painted over with the finest flowers.

" You poor little child ! " said the old woman, " how did you manage to come on the great rolling river, and to float thus far out into the world ? "

And then the old woman went quite into the water, seized the boat with her crutch-stick, drew it to land, and lifted little Gerda out. And Gerda was glad to be on dry land again, though she felt a little afraid of the strange old woman.

" Come and tell me who you are, and how you came here," said the old lady. And Gerda told her everything ; and the old woman shook her head, and said, " Hem ! hem ! " And when Gerda had told everything, and asked if she had not seen little Kay the woman said that he had not yet come by, but that he probably would soon come. Gerda was not to be sorrowful, but to look at the flowers and taste the cherries, for they were better than any picture-book, for each one of them could tell a story. Then she took Gerda by the hand and led her into the little house, and the old woman locked the door.

The windows were very high, and the panes were red, blue and yellow ; the daylight shone in a remarkable way, with different colours. On the table stood the finest cherries, and Gerda ate as many of them as she liked, for she had leave to do so. While she was eating them, the old lady combed her hair with a golden comb and the hair hung in ringlets of pretty yellow round the friendly little face, which looked as blooming as a rose.

" I have long wished for such a dear little girl as you," said the old lady. " Now you shall see how well we shall live with one another."

And as the ancient dame combed her hair, Gerda forgot her adopted brother Kay more and more ; for this old woman could conjure, but she was not a wicked witch. She only practised a little magic for her own amusement, and wanted to keep little Gerda. Therefore she went into the garden, stretched out her crutch towards all the rose-bushes, and, beautiful as they were, they all sank into the earth, and one could not tell where they had stood. The old woman was afraid that if the little girl saw roses, she would think of her own, and remember little Kay, and run away.

Now Gerda was led out into the flower-garden. What fragrance was there, and what loveliness ! Every conceivable flower was there in full bloom ; there were some for every season : no picture-book could be gayer and prettier, Gerda jumped high for joy, and played till the sun went down behind the high cherry-trees ; then she was put into a lovely bed with red silk pillows stuffed with blue violets, and she slept there, and dreamed as gloriously as a Queen on her wedding-day.

One day she played again with the flowers in the warm sunshine ; and thus many days went by. Gerda knew every flower ; but, as many as there were of them, it still seemed to her as if one were wanting, but which one she did not know. One day she sat looking at the old lady's hat with the painted flowers, and the prettiest of them all was a rose. The old lady had forgotten to take it out of her hat when she caused the others to disappear. But so it always is when one does not keep one's wits about one.

" What, are there no roses here ? " cried Gerda.

And she went among the beds, and searched and searched, but there was not one to be found. Then she sat down and wept: her tears fell just upon a spot where a rose-bush lay buried, and when the warm tears moistened the earth, the bush at once sprouted up as blooming as when it had sunk ; and Gerda embraced it, and kissed the Roses, and thought of the beautiful roses at home, and also of little Kay.

" Oh, how I have been detained ! " said the little girl. " I wanted to seek for little Kay ! Do you know where he is ? " she asked the Roses. " Do you think he is dead ? "

" He is not dead," the Roses answered. " We have been in the ground. All the dead people are there, but Kay is not there."

" Thank you," said little Gerda ; and she went to the other flowers, looked into their cups, and asked, " Do you not know where little Kay is ? "

But every flower stood in the sun thinking only of her own story or fairy tale : Gerda heard many, many of them ; but not one knew anything of Kay.

And what did the Tiger-Lily say ?

" Do you hear the drum ' Rub-dub ' ? There are only two notes, always ' rub-dub ! ' Hear the morning song of the women, hear the call of the priests. The Hindoo widow stands in her long red mantle on the funeral pile ; the flames rise up around her and her dead husband ; but the Hindoo woman is thinking of the living one here in the circle, of him whose eyes burn hotter than flames whose fiery glances have burned in her soul more ardently than the flames themselves, which are soon to burn her body to ashes. Can the flame of the heart die in the flame of the funeral pile ? "

" I don't understand that at all ! " said little Gerda.

" That's my story," said the Lily.

What says the Convolvulus ?

" Over the narrow road looms an old knightly castle : thickly the ivy grows over the crumbling red walls, leaf by leaf up to the balcony, and there stands a beautiful girl ; she bends over the balustrade and looks down at the road. No rose on its branch is fresher than she ; no apple blossom wafted onward by the wind floats more lightly along. How her costly silks rustle ! ' Comes he not yet ? ' "

" Is it Kay whom you mean ? " asked little Gerda.

" I'm only speaking of my own story—my dream," replied the Convolvulus.

What said the little Snowdrop ?

" Between the trees a long board hangs by ropes ; that is a swing. Two pretty little girls, with clothes white as snow and long green silk ribbons on their hats, are sitting upon it, swinging ; their brother, who is greater than they, stands in the swing, and has slung his arm round the rope to hold himself, for in one hand he has a little saucer, and in the other a clay pipe ; he is blowing bubbles. The swing flies and the bubbles rise with beautiful changing colours; the last still hangs from the pipe-bowl, swaying in the wind. The swing flies on : the little black dog, light as the bubbles, stands up on his hind legs and wants to be taken into the swing ; it flies on, and the dog falls, barks and grows angry, for he is teased, and the bubble bursts. A swinging board and a bursting bubble—that is my song."

"It may be very pretty, what you're telling, but you speak it so mournfully, and you don't mention little Kay at all."

What do the Hyacinths say?

"There were three beautiful sisters, transparent and delicate. The dress of one was red, that of the second blue, and that of the third quite white; hand in hand they danced by the calm lake in the bright moonlight. They were not elves, they were human beings. It was so sweet and fragrant there! The girls disappeared in the forest, and the sweet fragrance became stronger: three coffins with the three beautiful maidens lying in them, glided from the wood-thicket across the lake; the glow-worms flew gleaming about them like little hovering lights. Are the dancing girls sleeping, or are they dead? The flower-scent says they are dead and the evening bell tolls their knell."

"You make me quite sorrowful," said little Gerda. "You scent so strongly, I cannot help thinking of the dead maidens. Ah! is little Kay really dead? The roses have been down in the earth, and they say no."

"Kling! klang!" tolled the Hyacinth Bells. "We are not tolling for little Kay—we don't know him; we only sing our song, the only one we know."

And Gerda went to the Buttercup, gleaming forth from the green leaves.

"You are a little bright sun," said Gerda. "Tell me, if you know, where I may find my companion."

And the Buttercup shone so gaily, and looked back at Gerda. What song might the Buttercup sing? It was not about Kay.

"In a little courtyard the clear sun shone warm on the first day of spring. The sunbeams glided down in the white wall of the neighbouring house; close by grew the first yellow flower, glancing like gold in the bright sun's ray. The old grandmother sat out of doors in her chair; her granddaughter, a poor handsome maidservant, was coming home for a short visit: she kissed her grandmother. There was gold, heart's gold, in that blessed kiss, gold in the mouth, gold in the south, gold in the morning hour. See, that's my little story," said the Buttercup.

"My poor old grandmother!" sighed Gerda. "Yes, she is surely longing for me and grieving for me, just as she did for little Kay. But I shall soon go home and take Kay with me. There is no use of my asking the flowers, they only know their own song, and give me no information." And then she tied her little frock round her, that she might run the faster; but the Jonquil struck against her leg as she sprang over it, and she stopped to look at the tall yellow flower, and asked, "Do you perhaps, know anything of little Kay?"

And she bent quite down to the flower, and what did it say?

"I can see myself! I can see myself!" said the Jonquil. "Oh! oh! how I can smell! Up in the little room in the gable stands a little dancing girl: she stands sometimes on one foot, sometimes on both; she seems to tread on all the world. She's nothing but an ocular delusion: she pours water out of a teapot on a bit of stuff— it is her bodice. 'Cleanliness is a fine thing,' she says; her white frock hangs on a hook; it has been washed in the teapot too, and dried on the roof: she puts it on and ties her saffron handkerchief round her neck, and the dress looks all the whiter. Point your toes! look how she seems to stand on a stalk. I can see myself! I can see myself!"

"I don't care at all about that," said Gerda. "That is nothing to tell me about."

And then she ran to the end of the garden. The door was locked, but she pressed against the rusty lock, and it broke off, the door sprang open, and little Gerda ran with naked feet out into the wide world. She looked back three times, but no one was there to pursue her; at last she could run no longer, and seated herself on a great stone, and when she looked round the summer was over—it was late in autumn: one could not notice that in the beautiful garden, where there was always sunshine, and the flowers of every season always bloomed.

"Alas! how I have loitered!" said little Gerda. "Autumn has come. I may not rest again."

And she rose up to go on. Oh! how sore and tired her little feet were. All around it looked cold and bleak; the long willow leaves were quite yellow, and the mist dropped from them like water; one leaf after another dropped; only the sloe-thorn still bore fruit, but the sloes were sour, and set the teeth on edge. Oh! how grey and gloomy it looked, the wide world!

FOURTH STORY

The Prince and Princess

"Gerda was compelled to rest again; then there came hopping across the snow, just opposite the spot where she was sitting, a great Crow. This Crow had long been sitting looking at her, nodding its head—now it said, "Krah! krah! Good day! good day!" It could not pronounce better, but it felt friendly towards the little girl, and asked where she was going all alone in the wide world. The word "alone" Gerda understood very well, and felt how much it expressed; and she told the Crow the whole story of her life and fortunes, and asked if it had not seen Kay.

And the Crow nodded very gravely, and said,

"That may be! that may be!"

"What, do you think so?" cried the little girl, and nearly pressed the Crow to death, she kissed it so.

"Gently, gently!" said the Crow. "I think I know: I believe it may be little Kay, but he has certainly forgotten you, with the Princess."

"Does he live with a Princess ? " asked Gerda.

"Yes ; listen," said the Crow. "But it's so difficult for me to speak your language. If you know the Crows' language, I can tell it much better."

"No, I never learned it," said Gerda ; "but my grandmother understood it, and could speak the language too. I only wish I had learned it."

"That doesn't matter," said the Crow. "I shall tell you as well as I can."

And then the Crow told what he knew.

"In the country in which we now are, lives a Princess who is quite wonderfully clever, but then she has read all the newspapers in the world, and has forgotten them again, she is so clever. Lately she was sitting on the throne—and that's not so pleasant as is generally supposed—and she began to sing a song, and it was just this, ' Why should I not marry now ? ' You see, there was something in that," said the Crow. "And so she wanted to marry, but she wished for a husband who could answer when he was spoken to, not one who only stood and looked handsome, for that is so tiresome. And so she had all her maids of honour summoned, and when they heard her intention they were very glad. ' I like that,' said they ; ' I thought the very same thing the other day.' You may be sure that every word I am telling you is true," added the Crow. " I have a tame sweetheart who goes about freely in the castle, and she told me everything."

Of course the sweetheart was a crow, for one crow always finds out another, and birds of a feather flock together.

" Newspapers were published directly, with a border of hearts and the Princess's initials. One could read in them that every young man who was good-looking might come to the castle and speak with the Princess, and him who spoke so that one could hear he was at home there, and who spoke best, the Princess would choose for her husband. Yes, yes," said the Crow, " you may believe me. It's as true as I sit here. Young men came flocking in ; there was a great crowding and much running to and fro, but no one succeeded the first or second day. They could all speak well when they were out in the streets, but when they entered at the palace gates, and saw the guards standing in their silver lace and went up the staircase, and saw the lackeys in their golden liveries, and the great lighted halls, they became confused. And when they stood before the throne itself, on which the Princess sat, they could do nothing but repeat the last word she had spoken, and she did not care to hear her own words again. It was just as if the people in there had taken some narcotic and fallen asleep, till they got into the street again, for not till then were they able to speak. There stood a whole row of them, from the town gate to the palace gate. I went in myself to see it," said the Crow. " They were hungry and thirsty, but in the palace they did not receive so much as a glass of lukewarm water. A few of the wisest had brought bread and butter with them, but they would not share with their neighbours, for they thought 'Let him look hungry, and the Princess won't have him.'"

" But Kay, little Kay ? " asked Gerda. " When did he come ? Was he among the crowd ? "

" Wait, wait ! We're just coming to him. It was on the third day that there came a little personage, without horse or carriage, walking quite merrily up to the castle ; his eyes sparkled like yours, he had fine long hair, but his clothes were shabby."

" That was Kay ! " cried Gerda, rejoicingly. " Oh, then I have found him ! " And she clapped her hands.

" He had a little knapsack on his back " observed the Crow.

" No, that must certainly have been his sledge," said Gerda, "for he went away with a sledge."

"That may well be," said the Crow, "for I did not look to it very closely. But this much I know from my tame sweetheart, that when he passed under the palace gate and saw the Life Guards in silver, and mounted the staircase and saw the lackeys in gold, he was not in the least embarrassed. He nodded, and said to them, 'It must be tedious work standing on the stairs—I'd rather go in.' The halls shone full of lights; privy councillors and Excellencies walked about with bare feet, and carried golden vessels; any one might have become solemn; and his boots creaked most noisily, but he was not embarrassed."

"That is certainly Kay!" cried Gerda. "He had new boots on; I've heard them creak in grandmother's room."

"Yes, certainly they creaked," resumed the Crow. "And he went boldly to the Princess herself, who sat on a pearl that was as big as a spinning-wheel; and all the maids of honour with their attendants, and the attendants' attendants, and all the cavaliers with their followers, and the followers of their followers, who themselves kept a page apiece, were standing round; and the nearer they stood to the door, the prouder they looked. The followers' followers' pages, who always went in slippers, could hardly be looked at, so proudly did they stand in the doorway!"

"That must be terrible!" faltered little Gerda. "And yet Kay won the Princess?"

"If I had not been a crow, I would have married her myself, notwithstanding that I am engaged. They say he spoke as well as I can speak the crows' language; I heard that from my tame sweetheart. He was merry and agreeable; he had not come to woo, but only to hear the wisdom of the Princess; and he approved of her, and she of him."

"Yes, certainly that was Kay!" said Gerda. "He was so clever, he could do mental arithmetic up to fractions. Oh! won't you lead me to the castle too?"

THE SNOW QUEEN

"That's easily said," replied the Crow. "But how are we to manage it? I'll talk it over with my tame sweetheart; she can probably advise us; for this I must tell you—a little girl like yourself will never get leave to go quite in."

"Yes, I shall get leave," said Gerda. "When Kay hears that I'm there he'll come out directly, and bring me in."

"Wait for me yonder at the stile," said the Crow; and it wagged its head and flew away.

It was already late in the evening when the Crow came back.

"Rare! rare!" it said. "I'm to greet you kindly from my sweetheart, and here's a little loaf for you. She took it from the kitchen. There's plenty of bread there, and you must be hungry. You can't possibly get into the palace, for you are barefoot, and the guards in silver and the lackeys in gold would not allow it. But don't cry; you shall go up. My sweetheart knows a little back staircase that leads up to the bedroom, and she knows where she can get the key."

And they went into the garden, into the great avenue, where one leaf was falling down after another; and when the lights were extinguished in the palace one after the other, the Crow led Gerda to a back door, which stood ajar.

Oh, how Gerda's heart beat with fear and longing! It was just as if she had been going to do something wicked; and yet she only wanted to know if it was little Kay. Yes, it must be he. She thought so deeply of his clear eyes and his long hair, she could fancy she saw how he smiled as he had smiled at home when they sat among the roses. He would certainly be glad to see her; to hear what a long distance she had come for his sake; to know how sorry they had all been at home when he did not come back. Oh, what a fear and what a joy that was!

Now they were on the staircase. A little lamp was burning upon a cupboard, and in the middle of the floor stood the tame Crow turning her head on every side and looking at Gerda, who curtsied as her grandmother had taught her to do.

"My betrothed has spoken to me very favourably of you, my little lady," said the tame Crow. "Your history, as it may be called, is very moving. Will you take the lamp? then I will precede you. We will go the straight way, for we shall meet nobody."

"I feel as if some one were coming after us," said Gerda, as something rushed by her: it seemed like shadows on the wall; horses with flying manes and thin legs, hunters, and ladies and gentlemen on horseback.

"These are only dreams," said the Crow; "they are coming to carry the high masters' thoughts out hunting. That's all the better, for you may look at them the more closely, in bed. But I hope, when you come to honour and dignity, you will show a grateful heart."

"Of that you may be sure!" observed the Crow from the wood.

Now they came into the first hall: it was hung with rose-coloured satin, and artificial flowers were worked on the walls; and here the dreams already came flitting by them, but they moved so quickly that Gerda could not see the high-born lords and ladies. Each hall was more splendid than the last; yes, one could almost become bewildered! Now they were in the bedchamber. Here the ceiling was like a great palm-tree with leaves of glass, of costly glass, and in the middle of the floor two beds hung on a thick stalk of gold, and each of them looked like a lily. One of them was white, and in that lay the Princess; the other was red, and in that Gerda was to seek little Kay. She bent one of the red leaves aside, and then she saw a little brown neck. Oh, that was Kay! She called out his name quite loud, and held the lamp towards him. The dreams rushed into the room again on horseback—he awoke, turned his head, and—it was not little Kay!

The Prince was only like him in the neck! but he was young and good-looking, and the Princess looked up, blinking, from the white lily, and asked who was there. Then little Gerda wept, and told her whole history, and all that the Crows had done for her.

"You poor child!" said the Prince and Princess.

And they praised the Crows, and said that they were not angry with them at all, but the Crows were not to do it again. However they should be rewarded.

"Will you fly out free?" asked the Princess, "or will you have fixed positions as court crows, with the right to everything that is left in the kitchen?"

And the two Crows bowed, and begged for fixed positions, for they thought of their old age, and said, "It is so good to have some provisions for one's old days," as they called them.

And the Prince got up out of his bed, and let Gerda sleep in it, and he could not do more than that. She folded her little hands, and thought, "How good men and animals are!" and then she shut her eyes and went quietly to sleep. All the dreams came flying in again, looking like angels, and they drew a little sledge, on which Kay sat nodding; but all this was only a dream, and therefore it was gone again as soon as she awoke.

The next day she was clothed from head to foot in silk and velvet; and an offer was made her that she should stay in the castle and enjoy pleasant times; but she only begged for a little carriage, with a horse to draw it, and a pair of little boots; then she would drive out into the world and seek for Kay.

And she received not only boots, but a muff likewise, and was neatly dressed; and when she was ready to depart a coach made of pure gold stopped before the door. Upon it shone like a star the coat of arms of the Prince and Princess; coachman, footmen, and outriders—for there were outriders too—sat on horseback with gold crowns on their heads. The Prince and Princess themselves helped her into the carriage, and wished her all good fortune. The forest Crow, who was now married, accompanied her the first three miles; he sat by Gerda's side, for he could not bear riding backwards: the other Crow stood in the doorway flapping her wings; she did not go with them, for she suffered from headache, that had come on since she had obtained a fixed position and was allowed to eat too much. The coach was lined with sugar-biscuits, and in the seat there were gingerbread-nuts and fruit.

"Farewell, farewell!" cried the Prince and Princess; and little Gerda wept, and the Crow wept. So they went on for the first three miles; and then the Crow said good-bye, and that was the heaviest parting of all. The Crow flew up on a tree, and beat his black wings as long as he could see the coach, which glittered like the bright sunshine.

FIFTH STORY

The Little Robber Girl

They drove on through the thick forest, but the coach gleamed like a torch, dazzling the robbers' eyes, so that they could not bear it.

"That is gold! that is gold!" cried they, and rushed forward, and seized the horses, killed the postilions, the coachman, and the footmen, and then pulled little Gerda out of the carriage.

"She is fat—she is pretty—she is fed with nut-kernels!" said the old robber woman, who had a very long stiff beard, and shaggy eyebrows that hung down over her eyes. "She's as good as a little pet lamb; how I shall relish her!"

And she drew out her shining knife, that gleamed in a horrible way.

"Oh!" screamed the old woman at the same moment; for her own daughter who hung at her back bit her ear in a very naughty and spiteful manner. "You ugly brat!" screamed the old woman; and she had not time to kill Gerda.

"She shall play with me!" said the little robber girl. "She shall give me her muff and her pretty dress and sleep with me in my bed!"

And then the girl gave another bite, so that the woman jumped high up and turned right round, and all the robbers laughed and said,

"Look how she dances with her calf."

"I want to go into the carriage," said the little robber girl.

And she would have her own way, for she was spoiled, and very obstinate ; and she and Gerda sat in the carriage, and drove over stock and stone deep into the forest. The little robber girl was as big as Gerda, but stronger and more broad-shouldered ; and she had a brown skin ; her eyes were quite black, and they looked almost mournful. She clasped little Gerda round the waist, and said,

"They shall not kill you as long as I am not angry with you. I suppose you are a Princess ?"

"No," replied Gerda. And she told all that had happened to her, and how fond she was of little Kay.

The robber girl looked at her seriously, nodded slightly, and said,

"They shall not kill you even if I do get angry with you, for then I will do it myself."

And then she dried Gerda's eyes, and put her two hands into the beautiful muff that was so soft and warm.

Now the coach stopped, and they were in the courtyard of a robber castle. It had split from the top to the bottom ; ravens and crows flew out of the great holes, and big bulldogs—each of which looked as if he could devour a man—jumped high up, but they did not bark, for that was forbidden.

In the great old smoky hall a bright fire burned upon the stone floor ; the smoke passed along under the ceiling, and had to seek an exit for itself. A great cauldron of soup was boiling and hares and rabbits were roasting on the spit.

"You shall sleep to-night with me and all my little animals," said the robber girl.

They got something to eat and drink, and then went to a corner, where straw and carpets were spread out. Above these sat on laths and perches more than a hundred pigeons, that all seemed asleep, but they turned a little when the two girls came.

" All these belong to me," said the little robber girl ; and she quickly seized one of the nearest, held it by the feet, and shook it so that it flapped its wings. " Kiss it ! " she cried, and beat it in Gerda's face. " There sit the wood rascals," she continued, pointing to a number of laths that had been nailed in front of a hole in the wall. "Those are wood rascals, those two ; they fly away directly if one does not keep them well locked up. And here's my old sweetheart ' Ba.' " And she pulled out by the horn a Reindeer, that was tied up, and had a polished copper ring round its neck. " We're obliged to keep him tight, too, or he'd run away from us. Every evening I tickle his neck with a sharp knife, and he's very frightened at that."

And the little girl drew a long knife from a cleft in the wall, and let it glide over the Reindeer's neck ; the poor creature kicked out its legs, and the little robber girl laughed, and drew Gerda into bed with her.

" Do you keep the knife beside you while you're asleep ? " asked Gerda, and looked at it in rather a frightened way.

" I always sleep with my knife," replied the robber girl. " One does not know what may happen. But now tell me again what you told me just now about little Kay, and why you came out into the wide world."

And Gerda told it again from the beginning ; and the Wood Pigeons cooed above them in their cage, and the other pigeons slept. The little robber girl put her arm round Gerda's neck, held her knife in the other hand and slept so that one could hear her ; but Gerda could not close her eyes at all—she did not know whether she was to live or die.

The robbers sat round the fire, singing and drinking, and the old robber woman tumbled about. It was quite terrible for a little girl to behold.

Then the Wood Pigeons said " Coo ! coo ! we have seen little Kay. A white hen was carrying his sledge : he sat in the Snow Queen's carriage, which drove close by the forest as we lay in our nests. She blew upon us young pigeons, and all died except us two. Coo ! coo ! "

" What are you saying there ? " asked Gerda. " Whither was the Snow Queen travelling ? Do you know anything about it ? "

" She was probably journeying to Lapland, for there they have always ice and snow. Ask the Reindeer that is tied up with the cord."

" There is ice and snow yonder, and it is glorious and fine," said the Reindeer. " There one may run about free in great glittering plains. There the Snow Queen has her summer tent ; but her strong castle is up towards the North Pole, on the island that's called Spitzbergen."

" Oh, Kay, little Kay ! " cried Gerda.

" You must lie still," exclaimed the robber girl, " or I shall thrust my knife into your body."

In the morning Gerda told her all that the Wood Pigeons had said, and the robber girl looked quite serious, and nodded her head and said,

" That's all the same, that's all the same ! "

" Do you know where Lapland is ! " she asked the Reindeer.

" Who should know better than I ? " the creature replied, and its eyes sparkled in its head. " I was born and bred there ; I ran about there in the snow-fields."

" Listen ! " said the robber girl to Gerda. " You see all our men have gone away. Only mother is here still, and she'll stay : but towards noon she drinks out of the big bottle, and then sleeps for a little while ; then I'll do something for you."

Then she sprang out of bed, and clasped her mother round the neck and pulled her beard, crying

" Good morning my old nanny-goat." And her mother filliped

her nose till it was red and blue ; but it was all done for pure love.

When the mother had drunk out of her bottle and had gone to sleep upon it, the robber girl went to the Reindeer, and said,

" I should like very much to tickle you a few times more with the knife, for you are very funny then ; but it's all the same. I'll loosen your cord and help you out, so that you may run to Lapland; but you must use your legs well, and carry this little girl to the palace of the Snow Queen, where her playfellow is. You've heard what she told me, for she spoke loud enough and you were listening."

The Reindeer sprang up high for joy. The robber girl lifted little Gerda on its back, and had the forethought to tie her fast, and even to give her a little cushion as a saddle.

" There are your fur boots for you," she said, " for it's growing cold ; but I shall keep the muff, for that's so very pretty. Still, you shall not be cold, for all that : here's my mother's big mufflers— they'll just reach up to your elbows. Now your hands look just like my ugly mother's."

And Gerda wept for joy.

" I can't bear to see you whimper," said the little robber girl. " No, you just ought to look very glad. And here are two loaves and a ham for you, so you won't be hungry."

These were tied on the Reindeer's back. The little robber girl opened the door, coaxed in all the big dogs, and then cut the rope with her sharp knife, and said to the Reindeer,

" Now run, but take good care of the little girl."

And Gerda stretched out her hands with the big mufflers towards the little robber girl, and said, " Farewell ! "

And the Reindeer ran over stock and stone, away through the great forest, over marshes and steppes, as quick as it could go. The wolves howled and the ravens croaked. " Hiss ! hiss ! " it went in the air. It seemed as if the sky were flashing fire.

" Those are my old Northern Lights," said the Reindeer. " Look how they glow !" And then it ran on faster than ever, day and night.

The loaves were eaten, and the ham as well, and then they were in Lapland.

SIXTH STORY

THE LAPLAND WOMAN AND THE FINLAND WOMAN

At a little hut they stopped. It was very humble; the roof sloped down almost to the ground, and the door was so low that the family had to creep on their stomachs when they wanted to go in or out. No one was in the house but an old Lapland woman, cooking fish on a train-oil lamp; and the Reindeer told Gerda's whole history, but it related its own first, for this seemed to the Reindeer the most important of the two. Gerda was so exhausted by the cold that she could not speak.

" Oh, you poor things," said the Lapland woman, "you've a long way to run yet ! You must go more than a hundred miles into Finmark, for the Snow Queen is there, staying in the country, and burning Bengal lights every evening. I'll write a few words on a dried cod, for I have no paper, and I'll give you that as a letter to the Finland woman ; she can give you better information than I."

And when Gerda had been warmed and refreshed with food and drink, the Lapland women wrote a few words on a dried codfish, and telling Gerda to take care of it, tied her again on the Reindeer and the Reindeer sprang away. Flash ! flash ! it went high in the air ; the whole night long the most beautiful blue Northern Lights were burning.

And then they got to Finmark, and knocked at the chimney of the Finland woman, for she had not even a door.

There was such a heat in the chimney that the woman herself went about almost naked. She was little and very dirty. She at once loosened little Gerda's dress and took off the child's mufflers and boots ; otherwise it would have been too hot for her to bear.

Then she laid a piece of ice on the Reindeer's head, and read what was written on the codfish ; she read it three times, and when she knew it by heart, she popped the fish into the soup-cauldron, for it was eatable, and she never wasted anything.

Now the Reindeer first told his own history, and then little Gerda's ; and the Finland woman blinked with her clever eyes, but said nothing.

"You are very clever," said the Reindeer : "I know you can tie all the winds of the world together with a bit of twine : if the seaman unties one knot, he has a good wind ; if he loosens the second, it blows hard ; but if he unties the third and the fourth, there comes such a tempest that the forests are thrown down. Won't you give the little girl a draught, so that she may get twelve men's power, and overcome the Snow Queen ? "

"Twelve men's power ! " repeated the Finland woman. "Great use that would be ! "

And she went to a shelf, and brought out a great roll-up fur, and unrolled it ; wonderful characters were written upon it and the Finland woman read until the water ran down over her forehead.

But the Reindeer again begged so hard for little Gerda, and Gerda looked at the Finland woman with such beseeching eyes full of tears, that she began to blink again with her own, and drew the Reindeer into a corner, and whispered to him, while she laid fresh ice upon his head.

"Little Kay is certainly at the Snow Queen's, and finds everything there to his taste and liking, and thinks it the best place in the world ; but that is because he has a splinter of glass in his eye, and a little fragment in his heart ; but these must be got out, or he will never be a human being again, and the Snow Queen will keep her power over him."

"But cannot you give something to little Gerda, so as to give her power over all this ? "

" I can give her no greater power than she possesses already : don't you see how great that is ? Don't you see how men and animals are obliged to serve her, and how she gets on so well in the world, with her naked feet ? She must not learn her power from us : it consists in this, that she is a dear innocent child. If she herself cannot penetrate to the Snow Queen and get the glass out of little Kay, we can be of no use ! Two miles from here the Snow Queen's garden begins ; you can carry the little girl thither: set her down by the great bush that stands with its red berries in the snow. Don't stand gossiping, but make haste, and get back here ! "

And then the Finland woman lifted little Gerda on the Reindeer, which ran as fast as it could.

" Oh, I haven't my boots ! I haven't my mufflers ! " cried Gerda.

She soon noticed that in the cutting cold ; but the Reindeer dare not stop : it ran till it came to the bush with the red berries ; there it set Gerda down, and kissed her on the mouth, and great bright tears ran over the creature's cheeks ; and then it ran back, as fast as it could. There stood poor Gerda without shoes, without gloves, in the midst of the terrible cold Finmark.

She ran forward as fast as possible ! then came a whole regiment of snowflakes ; but they did not fall down from the sky, for that was quite bright, and shone with the Northern Lights : the snowflakes ran along the ground, and the nearer they came the larger they grew. Gerda still remembered how large and beautiful the snowflakes had appeared when she looked at them through the burning-glass. But here they were certainly far longer and much more terrible—they were alive. They were the advanced posts of the Snow Queen, and had the strangest shapes. A few looked like ugly great porcupines ; others like knots formed of snakes, which stretched forth their heads; and others like little fat bears, whose hair stood on end : all were brilliantly white, all were living snowflakes.

Then little Gerda said her prayer ; and the cold was so great that she could see her own breath, which went forth out of her mouth like smoke. The breath became thicker and thicker, and formed itself into little angels, who grew and grew whenever they touched the earth ; and all had helmets on their heads and shields and spears in their hands ; their number increased more and more, and when Gerda had finished her prayer a whole legion stood round about her and struck with their spears at the terrible snowflakes, so that these were shattered into a thousand pieces ; and little Gerda could go forward afresh, with good courage. The angels stroked her hands and feet, and then she felt less how cold it was, and hastened on to the Snow Queen's palace.

But now we must see what Kay is doing. He certainly was not thinking of little Gerda, and least of all that she was standing in front of the palace.

SEVENTH STORY

OF THE SNOW QUEEN'S CASTLE AND WHAT HAPPENED THERE AT LAST

The walls of the palace were formed of the drifting snow, and the windows and doors of the cutting winds. There were more than a hundred halls, all blown together by the snow : the greatest of these extended for several miles ; the strong Northern Lights illumined them all, and how great and empty, how icily cold and shining they all were ! Never was merriment there, not even a little bears' ball, at which the storm could have played the music, while the bears walked about on their hind legs and showed off their pretty manners ; never any little coffee gossip among the young lady white foxes. Empty, vast, and cold were the halls of the Snow Queen. The Northern Lights flamed so brightly that one could count them where they stood highest and lowest. In the midst of this immense empty snow hall was a frozen lake, which had burst into a thousand pieces ; but each piece was like the rest, so that it was a perfect work of art ; and in the middle of the lake sat the Snow Queen when she was at home, and then she said that she sat in the mirror of reason, and that this was the only one, and the best in the world.

Little Kay was quite blue with cold—indeed, almost black, but he did not notice it, for she had kissed the cold shudderings away from him ; and his heart was like a lump of ice. He dragged a few sharp flat pieces of ice to and fro, joining them together in all kinds of ways, for he wanted to achieve something with them. It was just like when we have little tablets of wood, and lay them together to form figures—what we call the Chinese puzzle. Kay also went and laid figures, and, indeed, very artistic ones. That was the icy game of reason. In his eyes these figures were very remarkable and of the highest importance ; that was because of the fragment of glass sticking in his eye. He laid out the figures so that they formed a word—but he could never manage to lay down the word as he wished to have it—the word " Eternity." And the Snow Queen had said,

" If you can find out this figure, you shall be your own master, and I will give you the whole world and a new pair of skates."

But he could not.

" Now I'll hasten away to the warm lands," said the Snow Queen. " I will go and look into the black pots " : these were the volcanoes, Etna and Vesuvius, as they are called. " I shall make them a little white ! That's necessary ; that will do the grapes and lemons good."

And the Snow Queen flew away, and Kay sat quite alone in the great icy hall that was miles in extent, and looked at his pieces of ice, and thought so deeply that cracks were heard inside him : he sat quite stiff and still, one would have thought that he was frozen to death.

Then it happened that little Gerda stepped through the great gate into the wide hall. Here reigned cutting winds, but she prayed a prayer, and the winds lay down as if they would have gone to sleep ; and she stepped into the great empty cold halls, and beheld Kay ; she knew him, and flew to him and embraced him, and held him fast, and called out,

" Kay, dear little Kay ! at last I have found you ! "

But he sat quite still, stiff and cold. Then little Gerda wept hot tears, that fell upon his breast ; they penetrated into his heart, they thawed the lump of ice, and consumed the little piece of glass in it. He looked at her, and she sang :

> Roses bloom and roses decay,
> But 'we the Christ-child shall see one day.

Then Kay burst into tears ; he wept so that the splinter of glass came out of his eye. Now he recognized her, and cried rejoicingly,

" Gerda, dear Gerda ! where have you been all this time ? And where have I been ? " And he looked all around him. " How cold it is here ! how large and empty ! "

And he clung to Gerda, and she laughed and wept for joy. It was so glorious that even the pieces of ice round about danced for joy ; and when they were tired and lay down, they formed themselves just into the letters of which the Snow Queen had said that if he found them out he should be his own master, and she would give him the whole world and a new pair of skates.

And Gerda kissed his cheeks, and they became blooming ; she kissed his eyes, and they shone like her own ; she kissed his hands and feet, and he became well and merry. The Snow Queen might now come home ; his letter of release stood written in shining characters of ice.

And they took one another by the hand, and wandered forth from the great palace of ice. They spoke of the grandmother, and of the roses on the roof ; and where they went the winds rested and the sun burst forth ; and when they came to the bush with the red berries, the Reindeer was standing there waiting : it had brought another young reindeer, which gave the children warm milk, and kissed them on the mouth. Then they carried Kay and Gerda, first to the Finnish woman, where they warmed themselves thoroughly in the hot room, and received instructions for their journey home, and then to the Lapland woman, who had made their new clothes and put their sledge in order.

The Reindeer and the young one sprang at their side, and followed them as far as the boundary of the country. There the first green sprouted forth, and there they took leave of the two reindeer and the Lapland woman. "Farewell!" said all. And the first little birds began to twitter, the forest was decked with green buds and out of it on a beautiful horse (which Gerda knew, for it was the same that had drawn her golden coach) a young girl came riding, with a shining red cap on her head and a pair of pistols in the holsters. This was the little robber girl, who had grown tired of staying at home, and wished to go first to the north, and if that did not suit her, to some other region. She knew Gerda at once, and Gerda knew her too ; and it was a right merry meeting.

"You are a fine fellow to gad about!" she said to little Kay. "I should like to know if you deserve that one should run to the end of the world after you ?"

But Gerda patted her cheeks, and asked after the Prince and Princess.

"The've gone to foreign countries," said the robber girl.

"But the Crow ?" said Gerda.

"Why the Crow is dead," answered the other. "The tame one has become a widow, and goes about with an end of black worsted thread round her leg. She complains most lamentably, but it's all talk. But now tell me how you have fared, and how you caught him."

And Gerda and Kay told their story.

"Snip-snap-snurre-basse-lurre !" said the robber girl.

And she took them both by the hand, and promised that if she ever came through their town, she would come up and pay them a visit. And then she rode away into the wide world. But Gerda and Kay went hand in hand, and as they went it became beautiful spring, with green and with flowers. The church bells sounded, and they recognized the high steeples and the great town : it was the one in which they lived ; and they went to the grandmother's door, and up the stairs, and into the room, where everything remained in its usual place. The big clock was going " Tick! tack!" and the hands were turning ; but as they went through the rooms they noticed that they had become grown-up people. The roses out on the roof gutter were blooming in at the open window, and there stood the little children's chairs, and Kay and Gerda sat each upon their own, and held each other by the hand. They had forgotten the cold empty splendour at the Snow Queen's like a heavy dream. The grandmother was sitting in God's bright sunshine, and read aloud out of the Bible, " Except ye become as little children, ye shall in no wise enter into the kingdom of God."

And Kay and Gerda looked into each other's eyes, and all at once they understood the old hymn—

> Roses bloom and roses decay,
> But we the Christ-child shall see one day.

There they both sat, grown up, and yet children—children in heart—and it was summer, warm, delightful summer.